"I don't know who I can trust. So is that why you're here, to rescue me?"

"Not exactly." But why the heck did Cal suddenly feel as if he wanted to do just that? Still, he wasn't about to let her off the hook. "Why did you lie about who your baby's father is?" he demanded.

Jenna blinked, and her eyes widened. "How did you know?"

"This morning my director called me into his office to demand an explanation as to why I slept with someone in my protective custody."

"Oh, I had no idea. How did he even find out?"

"Because we've been keeping tabs on you, Jenna."

"Me? Why? Why am I suddenly so important to the government?"

"Because it seems someone wants you dead. You've been placed back in my protective custody until you and your baby are safe."

4

DELORES FOSSEN

EXPECTING TROUBLE

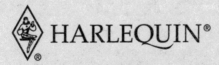

TORONTO • NEW YORK • LONDON
AMSTERDAM • PARIS • SYDNEY • HAMBURG
STOCKHOLM • ATHENS • TOKYO • MILAN • MADRID
PRAGUE • WARSAW • BUDAPEST • AUCKLAND

To Tom, thanks for all the support.

Recycling programs
for this product may
not exist in your area.

ISBN-13: 978-0-373-88890-0
ISBN-10:   0-373-88890-2

EXPECTING TROUBLE

ABOUT THE AUTHOR

Imagine a family tree that includes Texas cowboys, Choctaw and Cherokee Indians, a Louisiana pirate and a Scottish rebel who battled side by side with William Wallace. With ancestors like that, it's easy to understand why Texas author and former air force captain Delores Fossen feels as if she were genetically predisposed to writing romances. Along the way to fulfilling her DNA destiny, Delores married an air force top gun who just happens to be of Viking descent. With all those romantic bases covered, she doesn't have to look too far for inspiration.

Books by Delores Fossen

HARLEQUIN INTRIGUE

648—HIS CHILD
679—A MAN WORTH
    REMEMBERING
704—MARCHING ORDERS
727—CONFISCATED
    CONCEPTION
788—VEILED INTENTIONS
812—SANTA ASSIGNMENT
829—MOMMY UNDER COVER
869—PEEK A BOO BABY
895—SECRET SURROGATE
913—UNEXPECTED FATHER
932—THE CRADLE FILES
950—COVERT CONCEPTION
971—TRACE EVIDENCE
    IN TARRANT COUNTY
990—UNDERCOVER DADDY*

1008—STORK ALERT*
1026—THE CHRISTMAS CLUE*
1044—NEWBORN CONSPIRACY*
1050—THE HORSEMAN'S SON*
1075—QUESTIONING
    THE HEIRESS
1091—SECURITY BLANKET**
1110—BRANDED BY THE
    SHERIFF†
1116—EXPECTING TROUBLE†

*Five-Alarm Babies
**Texas Paternity
†Texas Paternity: Boots and Booties

CAST OF CHARACTERS

Cal Rico—This tough-as-nails agent faces his most important mission ever: he has to play daddy to a baby that everyone already believes is his. What Cal hadn't counted on was falling hard for the baby's mother and having to put his life on the line to protect them both.

Jenna Laniere—This Texas heiress's past comes back to haunt her, and to save her child she turns to Cal, even though an involvement with him—even a fake one—can destroy his career and send a deadly assassin gunning for him.

Sophie Laniere—Jenna's three-month-old daughter who's at the center of a dangerous game with the highest stakes.

Scott Kowalski—The director of the International Security Agency. He's Cal's boss, and he's not pleased that he has an agent personally involved with Jenna, a potential federal witness.

Mark Lynch—Cal's fellow agent and friend who might be selling secrets to the highest bidder.

Paul Tolivar—This cold-blooded businessman is dead, but he could have left deadly instructions for Sophie's kidnapping and Jenna's assassination.

Holden Carr—He inherited the bulk of Paul's estate, and he could be trying to eliminate anyone he sees as a threat to his inheritance. That includes Jenna and Sophie.

Anthony Salazar—A ruthless assassin who's after Jenna and her child. But who hired him?

Helena Carr—Holden's sister who claims she wants to stop her scheming brother, but she might have her own agenda.

Gwen Mitchell—A career-driven reporter who claims she's just after a story about Paul, but Gwen has some dangerous secrets of her own.

Prologue

A deafening blast shook the rickety hotel and stopped Jenna cold.

With her heart in her throat, Jenna raced to the window and looked down at the street below. Or rather what was left of the street, a gaping hole. Someone had set shops on fire. Black coils of smoke rose, smearing the late afternoon sky.

"Ohmygod," Jenna mumbled.

There was no chance a taxi could get to her now to take her to the airport. And worse were rebel soldiers, at least a dozen of them dressed in dark green uniforms. She'd heard about them on the news and knew they had caused havoc in Monte de Leon. That's why by now she'd hoped to be out of the hotel, and the small South American country. She hadn't succeeded because she'd been waiting on a taxi for eight hours.

One of the soldiers looked up at her and took aim with his scoped rifle. Choking back a scream, Jenna dropped to the floor just as the bullet slammed through the window.

She scurried across the threadbare rug and into the bathroom. It smelled of mold, rust and other odors she didn't want to identify, and Jenna wasn't surprised to see roaches race across the cracked tile. It was a far cry from the nearby Tolivar estate where she'd spent the past two days. Of course, there'd been insects of a different kind there.

Paul Tolivar.

Staying close to the wall, Jenna pulled off one of her red heels so she could use it as a weapon and climbed into the bathtub to wait for whatever was about to happen.

She didn't have to wait long.

There was a scraping noise just outside the window. She pulled in her breath and waited. Praying. She hadn't even made it to the please-get-me-out-of-this part when she heard a crash of glass and the thud of someone landing on the floor.

"I'm Special Agent Cal Rico," a man called out. "U.S. International Security Agency. I'm here to rescue you."

A rescue? Or maybe this was a trick by

one of the rebels to draw her out. Jenna heard him take a step closer, and that single step caused her pulse to pound in her ears.

"I know you're here," he continued, his voice calm. "I pinpointed you with thermal equipment."

The first thing she saw was her visitor's handgun. It was lethal-looking. As was his face. Lean, strong. He had an equally strong jaw. Olive skin that hinted at either Hispanic or Italian DNA. Mahogany-brown hair and sizzling steel-blue eyes that were narrowed and focused.

He was over six feet tall and wore all black, with various weapons and equipment strapped onto his chest, waist and thighs. He looked like the answer to her unfinished prayer.

Or a P.S. to her nightmare.

"We need to move now," he insisted.

Jenna didn't question that, but she still wasn't sure what she intended to do. Yes, she was afraid, but she wasn't stupid. "Can I trust you?"

Amusement leapt through his eyes. His reaction was brief, lasting barely a second before he nodded. And that was apparently all the reassurance he intended to give her. He latched on to her arm and hauled her from the tub. He allowed her just enough time to put back on her shoe before he maneuvered her out of the bathroom and toward the door to her hotel room.

"Extraction in progress, Hollywood," he whispered into a black thumb-size communicator on the collar of his shirt. "ETA for rendezvous is six minutes."

Six minutes. Not long at all. Jenna latched on to that info like a lifeline. If this lethal-looking James Bond could deliver what he promised, she'd be safe soon. Of course, with all those rebel soldiers outside, that was a big *if*.

Cal Rico paused at the door, listening, and eased it open. After a split-second glance down the hall, he got them out of the room and down a flight of stairs that took them to the back entrance on the bottom floor. Again, he looked out, but he must not have liked what he saw. He put his finger to his lips, telling her to stay quiet.

Outside, Jenna could still hear the battery of gunfire and the footsteps of the rebels. They seemed to be moving right past the hotel. She was in the middle of a battle zone.

How much her life had changed in two days. This should have been a weekend trip to Paul's Monte de Leon estate. A prelude to taking their relationship from friendship to something more. Instead, it'd become a terrifying ordeal she might not survive.

Jenna tried not to let fear take hold of her, but adrenaline was screaming for her to run. To do something. *Anything.* It was a powerful, overwhelming sensation. Fight or flight. Even if either of those options could get her killed.

Cal Rico touched his fingers to her lips. "Your teeth are chattering," he mouthed.

No surprise there. She didn't have a lot of coping mechanisms for dealing with this level of stress. Who did? Well, other than the guy next to her.

"Try doing some math," he whispered. "Or recite the Gettysburg Address. It'll help keep you calm."

Jenna didn't quite buy that. Still, she tried.

He moved back slightly. But not before she caught his scent. Sweat mixed with deodorant soap and the faint smell of the leather from his combat boots. It was far more pleasant than it should have been.

Stunned and annoyed with her reaction, Jenna cursed herself. Here she was, close to dying, only hours out of a really bad relationship, and her body was already reminding her that Agent Cal Rico smelled pleasant. Heaven help her. She was obviously a candidate for therapy.

"I'll do everything within my power to get you out of here," he whispered. "That's a promise."

Jenna stared at him, trying to figure out if he was lying. No sign of that. Just pure undiluted confidence. And much to her surprise, she believed him. It was probably a reaction to the testosterone fantasy he was weaving around her. But she latched on to his promise.

"All clear," he said before they started to move again.

They hurried out the door and into the alley that divided the hotel from another building. Cal never even paused. He broke into a run and made sure she kept up with him. He made a beeline for a deserted cantina. They ducked inside, and he pulled her to the floor.

"We're at the rendezvous point," he said into his communicator. "How soon before you can pick up Ms. Laniere?" A few seconds passed before he relayed to her, "A half hour."

That was an eternity with the battle raging only yards away. "We'll be safe here?" Jenna tried not to make it sound like a question.

"Safe enough, considering."

"How did you even know I was in that hotel?"

Cal shifted his position so he could keep watch out the window. "Intel report."

"There was an intelligence report about me?" But she didn't wait for him to answer. "Who are you? Not your name. I got that. But why are you here?"

He shrugged as if the answer were obvious. "I'm a special agent with International Security Agency—the ISA. I've been monitoring you since you arrived in Monte de Leon."

Still not understanding, she shook her head. "Why?"

"Because of your boyfriend, Paul Tolivar. He is bad news. A criminal under investigation."

Judas Priest. This was about Paul. Who else?

"My ex-boyfriend," she corrected. "And I wish I'd known he was bad news before I flew down here."

Maybe it was because she was staring craters into him, but Agent Rico finally looked at her. Their gazes met. And held.

"I don't suppose someone could have told me he was under investigation?" she demanded.

He was about to shrug again, but she held

tight to his shoulder. "We couldn't risk telling you because you might have told Paul."

Special Agent Rico might have added more, if there hadn't been an earsplitting explosion just up the street. It sent an angry spray of dirt and glass right at them. He reacted fast. He shoved her to the floor, and covered her body with his. Protecting her.

They waited. He was on top of her, with his rock-solid abs right against her stomach and one of his legs wedged between hers. Other parts of them were aligned as well.

His chest against her breasts. Squishing them.

The man was solid everywhere. Probably not an ounce of body fat. She'd never really considered that an asset, but she did now. Maybe all that strength would get them out of this alive.

Since they might be there for a while, and since Jenna wanted to get her mind off the gunfire, she forced herself to concentrate on something else.

"I believe Paul might be doing something illegal. He uses cash, never credit cards, and he always steps away from me whenever someone calls him on his cell. I know that's not really proof of any wrongdoing."

In fact, the only proof she had was that Paul was a jerk. When she refused to marry him, he'd slapped her and stormed out. Jenna hadn't waited around to see if he'd return with an apology. She hadn't even waited when Paul's driver had refused to take her into town. She'd walked the two miles, leaving everything but her purse behind.

Agent Rico smirked. "Tolivar was under investigation for at least a dozen felonies. The Justice Department thought you could be a witness for their case against him."

"Me?" She'd said that far louder than she intended. Then she whispered, "But I don't know anything." Oh, mercy. She hadn't thought things would be that bad. "What did Paul want with me? Not a green card. He's already a U.S. citizen."

Cal nodded. "The Justice Department believes he wanted your accounting firm so he could use it to launder money."

"Wait, he can't have my accounting firm. According to the terms of my father's will, I'm not allowed to sell or donate even a portion of the firm to anyone that isn't family."

He had no quick response, and his hesitation had her head racing with all sorts of bad ideas.

"We believe Paul Tolivar planned to marry

you one way or another this evening," Cal said. "He had a phony marriage license created, in case you turned down his proposal. Intel indicates that after the marriage, he planned to keep you under lock and key so he could control your business and your money."

A sickening feeling of betrayal came first. Then anger. Not just at Paul, but at herself for believing him and not questioning his motives. Still, something didn't add up. "If Paul planned to keep me captive, then why didn't he come after me when I left his estate?"

"He had someone follow you. I doubt he intended to let you leave the country. He contacted the only taxi service in town and told them to stall you."

So she'd been waiting for a taxi that would never have shown up. And it was probably just a matter of time before Paul came after her.

"I slept with him," Jenna mumbled. Groaned. She pushed her fists against the sides of her head. "You must think I'm the most gullible woman in the world."

"No. I think you're an heiress who was conned."

Yes. Paul had given her the full-court press after she'd met him at a fund-raiser.

Phone calls. Roses. *Yellow* roses, her favorite. And more. "He told me he was dying of a brain tumor."

Rico shook his head. "No brain tumor."

It took Jenna a moment to get her teeth unclenched. "The SOB. I want him arrested. I want—"

"He's dead."

She had to fight through her fit of rage to understand what he'd said. "Paul's dead?"

Cal Rico nodded. "He was murdered about an hour ago. That's why I'm here—to stop the same thing from happening to you."

Her heart fell to her knees. "Wh-what?"

"We have reason to believe that Paul left instructions. In the event of his death, he wanted others dead, too. You included. Those rebel soldiers out there are after you. And they have orders to kill you on sight."

Chapter One

*International Security Agency Regional
Headquarters
San Antonio, Texas
One year later*

Special Agent Cal Rico checked his watch—
again. Only three minutes had passed since
the last time he'd looked. It felt longer.

A lot longer.

Of course, waiting outside his director's
door had a way of making each second feel
like an eternity.

"Uh-oh," he heard someone say. Cal saw a
team member making his way up the hall
toward him. Mark Lynch was nicknamed
Hollywood because of his movie-star looks.
He was a Justice Department liaison assigned
to the regional headquarters. "What'd you
screw up, Chief?" Lynch asked.

Chief. Cal had been given his moniker because of his aspirations to become chief director of the International Security Agency. Except they weren't just aspirations. One day he *would* be chief. Since that was his one and only goal, it made things simple.

And in his mind, inevitable.

"Who said I screwed up anything?" Cal commented. But he was asking himself the same thing.

Lynch arched his left eyebrow and flashed a Tom Cruise smile. "You're outside Kowalski's office, aren't you?"

Cal had been assigned to the Bravo team of the ISA for well over a year, and this was the first time he'd ever been ordered to see his director. Since he'd just returned from a monthlong assignment in the Middle East and wouldn't receive new orders within seven duty days, he was bracing himself for bad news.

He'd already called his folks and both of his brothers to make sure all was well on the home front. That meant this had to do with the job. And that made it more personal than anything else could have been.

"If you have a butt left when Kowalski quits chewing it," Hollywood continued, "then show up at the racquetball court at 1730 hours. I believe you promised me a rematch."

Cal mumbled something noncommittal. He hated racquetball, but after this meeting he might need a way to work out some frustrations. Pounding Hollywood might just do it.

The door to the director's office opened, and Cal's lanky boss motioned for him to enter.

"Have a seat," Director Scott Kowalski ordered. There was no mistake about it. His tone and demeanor confirmed that it was an order. "Talk to me about Jenna Laniere."

Cal had geared up to discuss a lot of things with his boss, but she wasn't anywhere on that list. Though he'd certainly thought, and dreamed, about the leggy blond heiress. "What about her?"

"Tell me what happened when you rescued her in Monte de Leon last year."

That was a truly ominous-sounding request. Still, Cal tried not to let it unnerve him. "As best as I can recall, I entered the hotel where she'd checked in, found her hiding in the bathroom. I moved her from that location and got her to the rendezvous point. About a half hour later or so, the transport took her away, and I rejoined the Bravo team so we could extract some American hostages that the rebels had taken."

Kowalski put his elbows on his desk and leaned closer. "It's that half hour of unaccounted-for time that I'm really interested in."

Hell.

That couldn't be good. Had Jenna Laniere filed some kind of complaint all these months later? If so, Cal had her pegged all wrong. She had seemed too happy about being rescued to be concerned that he'd used profanity around her.

"Wait a minute," Cal mumbled, considering a different scenario. One that involved Paul Tolivar, or rather what was left of Tolivar's regime. "Is Jenna Laniere safe?"

Translation: had Tolivar's cronies or former business partners killed her?

The FBI had followed Jenna for weeks after her return to the States. When no one had attempted to eliminate her, they'd backed off from their surveillance.

As for Tolivar's regime, there hadn't been enough hard evidence for the Monte de Leon or U.S. authorities to arrest Tolivar's partners or anyone else for his murder. In fact, there hadn't been any evidence at all except for Justice Department surveillance tapes that couldn't be used in court since they would give away the identities of several deep-cover operatives. A move that would almost certainly cause the operatives to be executed. The Justice Department wasn't about to lose key men to further investigate a criminal's murder. Especially one that'd happened in a foreign country.

"Ms. Laniere's fine," Kowalski assured him.

The relief Cal felt was a little stronger than he'd expected. And it was short-lived. Because something had obviously happened. Something that involved her. If Jenna had indeed filed a complaint, there'd be an investigation. It could hurt his career.

The one thing he valued more than anything else.

He would not fail at this. He couldn't. Bottom line—being an operative wasn't his job, it was who he was. Without it, he was just the middle son of a highly decorated air force general. The middle son sandwiched between two brothers who'd already proven themselves a dozen times over. Cal had never excelled at anything. In his youth, he'd been average at best and at worst been a screwup— something his father often reminded him of.

His career in the ISA was the one way he could prove to his father, and more importantly to himself, that he was worth something.

"After you rescued Ms. Laniere, the Justice Department questioned her for hours. Days," Kowalski corrected. "She didn't tell them anything they could use to build their case against Tolivar's business partners. In fact, she claims she never heard Tolivar or his partners speak of the rebel group that they'd organized and funded in Monte de Leon. The group he ordered to kill her. She further claimed that she never heard him discuss his illegal activities."

"And the Justice Department believes she was telling the truth?"

Kowalski made a sound that could have meant anything. "Have you seen or spoken with her in the past year?"

"No." Cal immediately shook his head, correcting that. "I mean, I tried to call her about a month ago, but she wasn't at her office in Houston. I left a message on her voice mail, and then her assistant phoned back to let me know that she was on an extended leave of absence and couldn't be reached."

The director steepled his fingers and stared at Cal. "Why'd you try to call her?"

Cal leaned slightly forward as well. "This is beginning to sound a little like an interrogation."

"Because it is. Now back to the question—why did you make that call?"

Oh, man. That unnerving feeling that Cal had been trying to stave off hit him squarely between the eyes. This was not something he wanted to admit to his director. But he wouldn't lie about it, either.

No matter how uncomfortable it was.

"I was worried about her. Because I read the investigation into Tolivar's business partners had been reopened. I just wanted to see how things were with her."

Judging from the way Director Kowalski's smoke-gray eyes narrowed, that honest answer didn't please him. He muttered a four-letter word.

"Mind telling me what this is about?" Cal asked. "Because last I heard it isn't a crime for a man to call a woman and check on her."

But in this case, his director might consider it a serious error in judgment.

Since Jenna had a direct association with an international criminal like Paul Tolivar, no one working in the ISA should have considered her a candidate for a friendship. Or anything else.

Kowalski aimed an accusing index finger at Cal. "You know it violates regulations to have intimate or sexual contact with someone in your protective custody. And for those thirty minutes in Monte de Leon, Jenna Laniere was definitely in your protective custody."

That brought Cal to his feet. "Sexual contact?" Ah, hell. "Is that what she said happened?"

"Are you saying it didn't?"

"You bet I am. I didn't touch her." It took Cal a few moments to get control of his voice so he could speak. "Did she file a complaint or something against me?"

Kowalski motioned for him to take his seat again. "Trust me, Agent Rico, you'll want to sit down for this part."

Cal bit back his anger and sank onto the chair. Not easily, but he did it. And he forced himself to remain calm. Well, on the outside, anyway. Inside, there was a storm going on, and he could blame that storm on Jenna.

"As you know, I'm head of the task force assigned to clean up the problems in Monte de Leon," Kowalski explained. "The kidnapped American civilians. The destruction of American-owned businesses and interests."

Impatient with what had obviously turned into a briefing, Cal spoke up. "Is any of this connected to Ms. Laniere?"

"Yes. Apparently, she's still involved with Paul Tolivar's business partners. That's why we started keeping an eye on her again."

That took the edge off some of Cal's anger and grabbed his interest. "Involved—how?"

Kowalski pushed his hands through the sides of his graying brown hair. "She's been staying in a small Texas town, Willow Ridge, for the past couple of months. But prior to that while she was still in Houston, one of Tolivar's partners, Holden Carr, phoned her no less than twenty times. They argued. We're hoping that during one of their future conversations, Holden might divulge some information. That's why the Justice Department has been monitoring Ms. Laniere's calls and e-mails."

In other words, phone and computer taps. Not exactly standard procedure for someone who wasn't a suspected criminal. Of course, Hollywood would almost certainly have been aware of that surveillance and monitoring, and it made Cal wonder why the man hadn't at least mentioned it. Or maybe Hollywood hadn't remembered that Cal had rescued Jenna.

"What does all of this have to do with alleged sexual misconduct?" Cal insisted.

Kowalski hesitated a moment. Then two.

Just enough time to force Cal's anxiety level sky-high. "It's come to our attention that Jenna Laniere has a three-month-old daughter."

Oh, man.

It took Cal a few moments to find his breath, while he came up with a few questions that he was afraid even to ask.

"So what does that have to do with me?" Cal tried to sound nonchalant, but was sure he failed miserably.

"She claims the baby is yours."

Chapter Two

Cal finally spotted her.

Wearing brown pants and a cream-colored cable-knit sweater, Jenna came out of a small family-owned grocery store on Main Street. She had a white plastic sack clutched in each hand. But no baby.

One thing was for sure—she didn't look as if she'd given birth only three months earlier.

But she did look concerned. Her forehead was bunched up, and her gaze darted all around.

Good. She should be concerned about the lie she'd told. It probably wasn't a healthy thought to want to yell at a woman. But for the entire hour-long drive from regional headquarters to the little town of Willow Ridge, Texas, he'd played around with it.

She claims the baby is yours.

Director Kowalski's words pounded like fists in Cal's head. Powerful words, indeed.

Career-ruining words.

That's why he had to get this situation straightened out so that it couldn't do any more damage. Before the end of the week, he was due for a performance review, one that would be forwarded straight to the promotion board. If he had any hopes of making deputy director two years early, there couldn't even be a hint of negativity in that report.

And there wouldn't be.

That's what this visit was all about. One way or another, Jenna was going to tell the truth and clear his name. He'd worked too damn hard to let her take that early promotion away from him.

Cal stepped out of his car, ducked his head against the chilly February wind and strolled across the small parking lot toward her. He figured she was on her way to the apartment she'd rented over the town's lone bookstore. Judging from the direction she took, he was right.

Even though she kept close to the buildings, she was easy to track. Partly because there weren't many people out and about and partly because of her hair. Those shiny blond locks dipped several inches past her shoulders. Loose and free. The strands seemed to catch every ray of sun.

That hair would probably cause any man to give her a second look. Her body and face would cause a man to stare. Which was exactly what he was doing.

She must have sensed his eyes on her because she whirled around, her gaze snaring him right away.

"It's you," she said, squinting to see him in the harsh late afternoon sun. She sounded a little wary and surprised.

However, Cal's reactions were solely in the latter category.

First, there were her eyes. That shock of color. So green. So clear. He hadn't gotten a good look at her eyes when he rescued her in that dimly lit hotel, but he did now. And they were memorable. As was her face. She wore almost no makeup. Just a touch of peachy color on her mouth. She looked natural and sensual at the same time. But the most startling reaction of all was that he wasn't as angry at her as he had been five minutes before.

Well, until he forced himself to hang on to that particular feeling awhile longer.

"We have to talk," Cal insisted. And he wasn't about to let her say no. He took one of her grocery sacks so he could hook his arm through hers.

She looked down at the grip he had on her before she lifted her eyes to meet his. "This is about Paul Tolivar's business partner, isn't it? Is Holden Carr the one who's having me followed?"

That stopped Cal in his tracks. There was a mountain of concern in her voice and expression. Much to his shock, he wasn't immune to that concern.

He didn't like this feeling. The sudden need to protect her. This sure as heck wasn't an ISA-directed mission.

He repeated that to himself. "Someone is following you?" he asked.

She gave a surreptitious glance around, and since their arms were already linked, she maneuvered him into an alley that divided two shops.

"I spotted this man on my walk to the grocery store. He stayed in the shadows so I wasn't able to get a good look at him." Her words raced out, practically bleeding together. "Maybe he's following me, maybe he's not. And there's a reporter. Gwen

Mitchell. She introduced herself a couple of minutes ago in the produce aisle."

Cal made note of the name. Once he was done with this little chat, he'd run a background check on this Gwen Mitchell to see if she was legit. "What does she want?"

Jenna dismissed his question with a shrug, though tension was practically radiating from her. The muscles in her arm were tight and knotted. "She claims she's doing some kind of investigative report on Paul and the rebel situation in Monte de Leon."

That in itself wasn't alarming. There were probably lots of reporters doing similar stories because of the renewed investigation. "You don't believe her?"

"I don't know. Since the incident in Monte de Leon, I've been paranoid. Shadows don't look like shadows anymore. Hang-up calls seem sinister. Strangers in the grocery line look like rebel soldiers with orders to kill me." She shook her head. "And I'm sorry for dumping all of this on you. I know I'm not making any sense."

Unfortunately, she was making perfect sense. Cal had never met Paul's business partner, the infamous Holden Carr, but from what he'd learned about the man, Holden wasn't the sort to give up easily. Maybe he wanted to continue his late partner's quest to get Jenna's accounting firm and trust fund. Jenna's firm certainly wasn't the only one enticing to a potential money launderer, but Holden was familiar with it, and it had all the right foreign outlets to give him a quick turnover for the illegal cash.

Or maybe this was good news, and those shadows were Justice Department agents. Except Director Kowalski hadn't mentioned anything about her being followed. It was one thing to monitor calls and e-mails, but tailing a person required just cause and a lot of manpower. Since Jenna wasn't a suspect in a crime, there shouldn't have been sufficient cause for close surveillance.

And that brought them right back to Holden Carr.

"You've heard from Holden recently?" he asked. A lie detector of sorts since he knew from the director's briefing that she'd been in contact with the man in the past twenty-four hours.

"Oh, I've heard from him all right. Lucky me, huh? He's called a bunch of times, and right after I got back from Monte de Leon, he visited my office in Houston. And get this—

he says he's always been in love with me, that he wants to be part of my life. Right. He's in love with my estate and accounting firm, and what he really wants is to be part of my death so he can inherit it." She paused. "Please tell me he'll be arrested soon."

"Soon." But Cal had no idea if that was even true.

"Good. Because as long as he's a free man, I'm not safe. That's why I left Houston. I thought maybe if I came here, Holden wouldn't be able to find me. That he'd stop harassing me. Then yesterday afternoon he called me again, on my new cell phone." She moistened her lips. And looked away. "He threatened me."

That didn't surprise Cal. Holden wouldn't hesitate to resort to intimidation to get what he wanted. Still, that was a problem for the back burner. He had something more pressing.

"Holden didn't make an overt threat," Jenna continued before Cal could speak. "He implied it. It scared me enough to decide that I need professional security. A bodyguard or something. But I don't know anyone I can trust. I don't know if the bodyguard I call might really be working for Holden."

Unfortunately, that was a real possibility.

If Holden knew where she was, then he would also know how to get to her.

She paused and blew out a long breath. "Okay, that's enough about me and my problems. Why are you here?" She conjured a halfhearted smile. "Gosh, that's a déjà vu kind of question, isn't it? I remember asking you something similar when you were rescuing me in Monte de Leon. Is that why you're here now—to rescue me?"

"No." But why the heck did he suddenly feel as if he wanted to do just that?

From that still panicked look in her eyes, it wasn't a good time to bring up his anger, but Cal wasn't about to let her off the hook, either.

"Why did you lie about who your baby's father is?" he demanded.

Jenna blinked, and then her eyes widened. "How did you know?"

"Well, it wasn't a lucky guess, that's for sure. This morning my director called me into his office to demand an explanation as to why I slept with someone in my protective custody."

"Ohmygod." Jenna leaned against the wall and pulled in several hard breaths. "I had no idea. How did your director even find out I'd had a baby?"

Because she already had a lot to absorb,

Cal skipped right over the Justice Department eavesdropping on her, and gave her a summary of what Director Kowalski had relayed to him. "You told Holden Carr that the baby was mine."

Jenna nodded, and with her breath now gusting hard and fast, she studied his expression. It was as icy as the Antarctic. "This could get you into trouble, couldn't it?"

"It's *already* gotten me into trouble. Deep trouble. And it could get worse."

He would have added more, especially the part about Director Kowalski demanding DNA proof that Cal wasn't the baby's father. But he caught some movement from the corner of his eye. A thin-faced man in a dark blue two-door car. He drove slowly past them.

"That's the guy," Jenna whispered, tugging on the sleeve of Cal's leather jacket. "He's the one who followed me to the grocery store."

The words had hardly left her mouth when the man gunned the engine and sped away. But not before Cal made eye contact with him.

Oh, hell.

Cal recognized him from the intel surveillance photos.

He cursed, dropped the grocery bag and slipped his hand inside his jacket in case he had to draw his gun. "How long did you say he's been following you?"

Jenna shook her head and looked to be on the verge of panicking. "I think just today. Why? Do you know him? Is he a friend of yours?"

There was way too much hope in her voice.

"Not a friend," Cal assured her. "But I know *of* him." He left it at that. "Where's your baby?"

"In the apartment. My landlord's daughter is watching her. Why?"

Cal didn't answer that. "Come on. We'll finish this conversation there."

And once they had finished the discussion about the paternity of her child, he'd move on to some security measures he wanted her to take. Maybe the Justice Department could even provide her with protection or a safe house. He'd call Hollywood and Director Kowalski and put in a request.

Cal tried to get her moving, but Jenna held her ground. "Tell me—who's that man?"

Okay, so that wasn't panic in her eyes. It was determination. She wasn't about to drop this. Not even for a couple of minutes until they could reach her apartment.

"Anthony Salazar," Cal let her know. "That's his real name, anyway. He often uses an alias."

She stared at him. "He works for Holden Carr?"

"He usually just works for the person who'll pay him the most." Cal hadn't intended to pause, but he had to so he could clear his throat. "He's a hired assassin, Jenna."

Chapter Three

Jenna was glad the exterior wall of the café was there to support her, or her legs might have given way.

First, there was Cal's out-of-the-blue visit to deal with.

Then the news that he knew about the lie she'd told.

And now this.

"An assassin?" she repeated.

Somehow she managed to say aloud the two little words that had sent her world spinning out of control—again. She'd had a lot of that lately and was more than ready for it to stop.

Cal cursed under his breath. He picked up the grocery bag he'd dropped and then slipped his arm around her waist.

Jenna thought of her baby. Of Sophie. She couldn't let that assassin get anywhere near her daughter.

She started to break into a run, but Cal maneuvered her off the sidewalk and behind the café. They walked quickly into the alley that ran the entire length of Main Street. So they'd be out of sight.

"You didn't know that guy was here?" she asked as they hurried.

"No."

That meant Cal had come to confront her about naming him as Sophie's father. That alone was a powerful reason for a visit. She owed him an explanation.

And a Texas-size apology.

But for now, all Jenna wanted to do was get inside her apartment and make sure that hired gun, Anthony Salazar, was nowhere near her baby. And to think he might have been following her on her entire walk to the grocery store. Or even longer. He could have taken out a gun and fired at any time, and there wouldn't have been a thing she could do to stop it.

He could have hurt Sophie.

Maybe because she was shaking now, Cal tightened his grip around her, pulling her deeper into the warmth of his arm, while increasing the pace until they were jogging.

"I didn't name you as my baby's father to hurt your career," she assured him. "I didn't think anyone other than Holden would hear what I was saying."

A deep sound of disapproval rumbled in Cal's throat. He didn't offer anything else until they reached the bookstore. Her apartment was at the back and up the flight of stairs on the second floor.

"You have a security system?" he asked as they hurried up the steps.

"Yes."

She unlocked the door—both locks— tossed the groceries and her purse on the table in the entry and bolted across the room. The sixteen-year-old sitter, Manda, was on the sofa reading a magazine. Jenna raced past her to the bedroom and saw Sophie sleeping in her crib. Exactly where she'd left her just a half hour earlier at the start of her afternoon nap.

"Is something wrong?" Manda asked, standing.

Jenna didn't answer that. "Did anyone come by or call?"

Manda shook her head, obviously concerned. "Are you okay?"

"Fine," Jenna lied. "I just had a bad case of baby separation. I had to get back and make sure Sophie was all right. And she is. She's sleeping like…well, a baby."

Still looking concerned, Manda nodded, and her gaze landed on Cal.

"He's an old friend," Jenna explained. She purposely didn't say Cal's name. Best not to give too much information until she knew what was going on. Besides, she'd already caused Cal enough trouble.

Jenna took the twenty-dollar bill from her pocket and handed it to Manda. "But I was barely here thirty minutes," the teen protested. "Five bucks an hour, remember?"

"Consider the rest a tip." Jenna put her hand on Manda's back to get her moving. She needed some privacy so she could find out what was going on.

"Why didn't the alarm go off when we came in?" he wanted to know as soon as Manda walked out with her magazine tucked beneath her arm. It wasn't a question, exactly. More like the start of a cross-examination.

"It's connected to the bookstore." She shut the door and locked it. "The owner turns it on when she closes for the evening."

That didn't please him. His disapproving gaze fired around the apartment, but it didn't have to too far. It was one large twenty-by-twenty-five-foot room with an adjoining bath and a tiny nursery. The kitchenette and dining area were on one side, and the living room with its sofa bed was on the other. It wasn't exactly quaint and cozy with the vaulted, exposed beam ceiling, but it was a far cry from her massive family home near Houston.

"Why this place?" he asked after he'd finished his assessment.

"It has fewer shadows," she said, not wanting to explain about her sudden fear of bogeymen, assassins and rebel fighters.

She could still hear the bullets.

She'd always be able to hear them.

Cal nodded and eased the grocery bag onto the tile-topped table.

"You want a drink or something?" Jenna motioned to the fridge.

"No, thanks." There was an unspoken warning at the end of that. That was her cue to start explaining this whole baby-daddy issue.

She was feeling light-headed and was still shivering, so Jenna snagged the trail mix from her grocery bag and went to the sofa so she could sit down.

"First of all, I didn't know what I said about the baby would even get back to you. To anyone." She popped a cashew into her mouth and offered him some from the bag. He shook his head. "Yesterday, when Holden called, I'd just returned from Sophie's three-month checkup with the pediatrician. Right away, he started yelling, saying that he knew that I'd had a child."

"How did he know?"

"That's the million-dollar question." But then, Jenna rethought that. "Or maybe not. I stopped by my house on the outskirts of Houston to pick up some things before I went to the appointment. Holden probably had someone watching the place and then followed me. I was careful. You know, always checking the rearview mirror and the parking lot at the clinic. But he could have had that Salazar guy following me the whole time."

In hindsight, she should have anticipated Holden would do something like this. In fact, she should have known he would. He was as tenacious as he was ruthless.

"So Holden confronted you about the baby?" Cal asked.

"Oh, yes. Complete with yelling obscenities. And that was just the prelude. No more facade of being in love with me. He demanded to know if Paul was Sophie's father. If so, he said he would challenge me for custody."

"Custody?" Cal didn't hide his surprise very well.

"Apparently, Paul had some kind of provision in his will that would make Holden the legal guardian to any child that Paul might have—if I'm proven unfit, which Holden says he can do with his connections. After he threatened me with that, I stalled him, trying to think of what I should say, and your message was still in my head. It made the leap from my brain to my mouth before I could stop it, and I just blurted out your name."

Cal walked closer and slid onto the chair across from her. Close enough for her to see all the scorching blue in his eyes. And close enough to see the emotion and the anger, too. "My message?"

She swallowed hard. "The one you left on my voice mail at my office about a month ago. My assistant sent it to me, and I'd recently listened to it."

A lot. In fact, she'd memorized it.

She'd found his voice comforting, and that's why she'd replayed it. Night after night. When she couldn't sleep. When the nightmares got the best of her. But his voice wasn't comforting now, of course. Coupled with his riled glare, there wasn't much comforting about him or this visit.

Well, except that he'd put his arm around her when he thought she was cold.

A special kind of special agent.

He still looked the part, even though he wasn't in battle gear today. He wore jeans, a dark blue button-down shirt that was almost the same color as his eyes and a black leather jacket.

"Anyway, after I realized it was stupid to give Holden your name," she continued, "I thought about calling him back and making something up. But I figured that'd only make him more suspicious."

Because Cal wasn't saying anything and because she suddenly didn't know what to do with her hands, Jenna offered him the trail mix again, and this time he reached into the bag and took out a few pieces.

"I've done everything to keep my pregnancy and delivery quiet. *Everything*," Jenna said, aware that her nerves were causing her to babble. It was either that, humming or reciting something, and she didn't want to launch into a neurotic rendition of the Preamble to the Constitution. "I don't have any family, and none of my friends know. No one here in Willow Ridge really knows who I am, either."

She didn't think it was her imagination that he was hesitant to say anything. Under the guise of eating trail mix, Cal sat there, letting her babble linger between them.

Since she had to know what was going on in his head, Jenna just went for the direct approach. "How did your director find out that I'd told Holden about my baby?"

His jaw muscles began to stir against each other. "The Justice Department has kept tabs on you."

"Tabs?" She took a moment to consider that. "That's an interesting word. What does it mean exactly?"

More jaw muscles moved. "It means they were keeping track of you in case Holden decided to divulge anything incriminating they could use in their case against him."

So it was true. Her fears weren't all in her head. The authorities thought Holden might be a danger as well.

Or maybe they didn't.

Maybe they were just hoping Holden would do something stupid so they could use that to arrest him.

"I was bait?" she asked.

"No." But then he lifted his shoulder. "At least I don't think so."

Jenna prayed that was true. The thought wasn't something she could handle right now.

"The baby is Paul Tolivar's?" Cal asked.

She nodded. And waited for his reaction. She didn't get one. He put on his operative's face again. "Just how much trouble will this cause for you?" she wanted to know.

"The ISA has a morality clause." His fingers tightened around a dried apricot, squishing it. "Plus, the regs forbid personal contact during a protective custody situation."

That was not what she wanted to hear. "You could be punished."

Again, it took him a moment to answer. "Yeah."

"Okay." Jenna took a deep breath, and because she couldn't stay still, she got up to pace. There was a solution to this. Not necessarily an appetizing solution, but it did exist. "Will my statement that I lied be enough to clear you, or will you need a paternity test?"

"My director wants a test." He stood as well, and caught her arm when she started to go past him. His fingers were warm. Surprisingly warm. She could feel his touch all the way through her thick sweater. "But I think that's the least of your worries right now."

"Because of Anthony Salazar." Jenna nodded. "Yes. He's definitely a worry. His being here means I'll need to leave Willow Ridge and go into hiding."

"You're already in hiding," Cal pointed out. "And he found you. He'll find you again. He's very good at what he does. You need more protection than a bookstore security system or a hired bodyguard can give you. I'll make some calls and see what I can do."

Pride almost caused her to decline his offer. But she knew that it wouldn't protect her baby. And that was the most important thing right now. She had to stay safe because if anything happened to her, it would happen to her precious daughter as well.

"Thank you," Jenna whispered. She repeated it to make sure he heard her. "I really am sorry about dragging you into my personal life."

"We'll get it straightened out," he assured her. But there was a lot of skepticism in his voice.

And annoyance, which she deserved.

"Okay, while you make those calls, I'll arrange to have the paternity test done," Jenna added.

Somehow, though, she'd have to keep the

results a secret from anyone but Cal and his director.

Because she didn't want Holden to learn the truth. Jenna moved away from Cal and started to pace again, mumbling a poem she'd memorized in middle school. She couldn't help it. A few lines came out before she could stop them.

"What you must think of me," she said. "For what it's worth, Paul and I only had sex once, and we used protection. But I guess something went wrong…on a lot of levels. Honestly, I don't really even remember sleeping with him." Jenna mumbled that last part.

"You don't remember?" he challenged.

She shook her head. "One minute we were having dinner, and the next thing I remember was waking up in bed with him. I obviously had too much to drink. Or else he drugged me. Either way, it was my stupid mistake for being there. Then I made things so much worse by telling Holden that you're my daughter's father. And here we didn't even have sex. Heck, we never even kissed on the floor of that cantina."

A clear image formed in her mind. Of that floor. Of Cal on top of her to protect her from the explosion. It wasn't exactly pleasurable. Okay, it was. But it wasn't supposed to be.

Not then.

Not now.

She'd already done enough damage to Cal's career without her adding unwanted sexual attraction that could never go beyond the fantasy stage.

He opened his mouth to say something, but didn't get past the first syllable. There was a knock at the door, the sudden sound shattering the silence.

Cal reacted fast. He reached inside his jacket and pulled out a handgun from a shoulder holster. He motioned for her to move out of the path of the door.

Jenna raced across the room and took a knife from the cutlery drawer. It probably wouldn't give them much protection, but she didn't intend to let Cal fight alone. Especially since the battle was hers.

With his hands gripped around his weapon, he eased toward the door. Every inch of his posture and demeanor was vigilant. Ready. Lethal.

Cal didn't use the peephole to look outside, but instead peered out the corner of the window.

He cursed softly.

"It's Holden Carr."

Chapter Four

This was not how Cal had planned his visit.

It was supposed to be in and out quickly. He was only on a fact-finding mission so he could get out of hot water with the director. Instead, he'd walked right into a vipers' nest. And one viper was way too close.

Holden Carr was literally pounding on Jenna's door.

Cal glanced back at her. With a butcher knife in a white-knuckled death grip, Jenna was standing guard in front of the nursery. She was pale, trembling and nibbling on her bottom lip. *Bam!* There were his protective instincts.

There was no way he could let her face Holden Carr alone. From everything Cal had read about the man, Holden was as dangerous as Paul, his former business partner. And Paul had been ready to commit murder to get his hands on Jenna's estate.

"Go to your daughter," Cal instructed while Holden continued to pound.

She shook her head. "You might need backup."

He lifted his eyebrow. She wasn't exactly backup material. Jenna Laniere might have been temporarily living in a starter apartment in a quaint Texas cowboy town, but her blue blood and pampered upbringing couldn't have prepared her for the likes of Holden Carr.

"I'll handle this," Cal let her know, and he left no room for argument.

She mumbled something, but stepped back into the nursery.

With his SIG Sauer drawn, Cal stood to the side of the door. It was standard procedure— bad guys often like to shoot through doors. But Holden probably didn't have that in mind. It was broad daylight and with the door-pounding, he was probably drawing all kinds of attention to himself, but Cal didn't want to take an unnecessary risk.

Once he was in place, he reached over. Unlocked the door. And eased it open.

Cal jammed his gun right in Holden's face.

Holden's dust-gray eyes sliced in the direction of the SIG Sauer. There was just a flash of shock and concern before he buried those reactions in the cool composure of his Nordic pale skin and his Viking-size body. He was decked out in a pricy camel-colored suit that probably cost more than Cal made in a month.

"I'm Holden Carr and I need to see Jenna," he announced.

Cal didn't lower his gun. In fact, he jabbed it against Holden's right cheek. "Oh, yeah? About what?"

"A private matter."

"It's not so private. From what I've heard you're threatening her. It takes a special kind of man to threaten a woman half his size. Of course, you're no stranger to violence, are you? Did you murder Paul Tolivar?"

Holden couldn't quite bury his anger fast enough. It rippled through his jaw muscles and his eyes. "Who the hell are you?"

"Cal Rico. I'm Jenna's…friend." But he let his tone indicate that he was the man who wouldn't hesitate to pull the trigger if Holden tried to barge his way in. "Anything you have to say to Jenna, you can say to me. I'll make sure she gets the message."

"The message is she can't hide from me forever." Holden enunciated each word. "I know she had a baby. A little girl named

Sophie Elizabeth. Born three months ago. That means the child is Paul's."

It didn't surprise Cal that Holden knew all of this, but what else did he know? "Paul, the man you murdered," Cal challenged.

There was another flash of anger. "Not that it's any of your business, but I didn't murder him. His housekeeper did. She was secretly working for a rebel faction who had issues with some of Paul's businesses."

"Right. The housekeeper." Cal made sure he sounded skeptical. He'd already heard the theory of the runaway housekeeper known only as Mary. "I don't suppose she confessed."

Holden had to get his teeth apart before he could respond. "She fled the estate after she killed him. No one's been able to find her."

"Convenient. Now, mind telling me how you came by this information about Jenna's child?"

"Yes. I mind."

Cal hadn't expected him to volunteer that, since it almost certainly involved illegal activity. "Hmmm. I smell a wire tap. That kind of illegal activity can get you arrested. Your dual citizenship won't do a thing to protect you, either. If you hightail it back to Monte de Leon, you can be extradited."

Though that wasn't likely. Still, Cal made a note to discover the source of that possible tap.

Holden looked past him, and because they were so close, Cal saw the man's eyes light up. Cal didn't have to guess why. Holden was aiming his attention in the direction of the nursery door and had probably spotted Jenna. He tried to come inside, but Cal blocked the door with his foot.

"She'll have to talk to me sooner or later," Holden insisted. "Call off your guard dog," he yelled at Jenna.

"What do you want?" Jenna asked. Cal silently groaned when he heard her walking closer. She really didn't take orders very well.

"I want you to carry out Paul's wishes. In his will, he named me guardian of his children. He didn't have any children at the time he wrote that, but he does now."

"You only want my daughter so you can control me," Jenna tossed out.

Holden didn't deny it. "I've petitioned the court for custody," he said.

Jenna stopped right next to Cal, and she reached across his body to open the door wider. "No judge would give you custody."

"Maybe not in this country, but in Monte

de Leon, the law will be on Paul's side. Even in death he's still a powerful man with powerful friends."

"Sophie's an American," Jenna pointed out. "Born right here in Texas."

"And you think that'll stop Paul's wishes from being carried out? It won't. If the Monte de Leon court deems you unfit—and that can easily happen with the right judge—then the court will petition for the child to be brought to her father's estate."

"Sophie is not Paul's child." She looked Holden right in the eye when she told that lie.

But Holden only smiled. "I've seen pictures of her. She looks just like him. Dark brown hair. Blue eyes."

Pictures meant he had surveillance along with taps. This was not looking good.

Cal could hear Jenna's breath speed up. Fear had a smell, and she was throwing off that scent, along with motherly protection vibes. But that wouldn't do anything to convince this SOB that he didn't have a right to claim her child.

From the corner of his eye, Cal spotted a movement. There was a tall redheaded woman with a camera. She was about forty yards away across the street and was clicking pictures of this encounter. Gwen Mitchell no doubt. And she wasn't the only woman there. He also spotted a slender blonde making her way up the steps to Jenna's apartment.

"That's Helena Carr," Jenna provided.

Holden's sister and business partner. Great. Now there was an added snake to deal with, and it was all playing out in front of a photographer with questionable motives. Cal could already hear himself having to explain why he was in small-town America with his standard-issue SIG Sauer smashed against a civilian's face.

"This meeting is over," Cal insisted. He lowered his gun, but he kept it aimed at Holden's right kneecap.

"It'll be over when Jenna admits that her daughter is Paul's," Holden countered.

"We just want the truth." That from Helena, who was a feminine version of her brother without the Viking-wide shoulders. Her stare was different, too. Nonthreatening. Almost serene. "After all, we know she slept with Paul, and the timing is perfect to have produced Sophie."

Cal hoped he didn't regret this later, but there was one simple way to diffuse this. "I have dark brown hair, blue eyes. Just like

Sophie's." He hoped, since he hadn't actually seen the little girl.

Helena blinked and gave him an accusing stare. Holden cursed. "Are you saying you're the father?" he asked.

"No," Jenna started to say. But Cal made sure his voice drowned her out.

"Yes," Cal snarled. "I'm Sophie's father."

"Impossible," Holden snarled back.

Cal gave him a cocky snort. "There is nothing impossible about it. I'm a man. Jenna's a woman. Sometimes men and women have sex, and that results in a pregnancy."

And just in case Jenna was going to say something to contradict him, Cal gave her a quick glance. She was staring at him as if he'd lost his mind.

"You won't mind taking a DNA test," Holden insisted.

"Tell you what. You send the request for a DNA sample through your foreign judge and let it trickle its way through our American judicial system. Then I'll get back to you with an answer."

Of course, the answer would be no.

Still, that wouldn't stop Holden from trying. If he controlled Jenna's child, then he would ultimately have access to a vast money-laundering enterprise. Then he could fully operate his own family business and the one he'd inherited from Paul.

"This isn't over." Holden aimed the threat at Jenna as he stalked away.

Cal was about to shut the door and call his director so he could start some damage control, but Helena eased her hand onto the side to stop it from closing.

"I'm sorry about this." Helena sounded sincere. Or else she'd rehearsed it enough to fake sincerity. Maybe this was the brother-sister version of good cop/bad cop. "I just want the truth so I can make sure Paul's child inherits what she deserves."

Jenna didn't even address that. "Can you stop your brother?"

Cal carefully noted Helena's reaction. She glanced over her shoulder. First, at her brother who was getting inside their high-end car. Then at the photographer.

"Could I step inside for just a moment?" That sincerity thing was there again.

But Cal wasn't buying it.

Jenna apparently did. With the butcher knife still clutched in her hand, she stepped back so Helena could enter.

"That reporter out there might have some

way to eavesdrop on us," Helena explained. "She has equipment and cameras with her."

Maybe. But Cal hadn't seen anything to suggest long-range eavesdropping equipment. Still, it was an unnecessary risk to keep talking in plain view. Lipreading was a possibility. Plus, anything said here could ultimately put Jenna in more danger and get him in deeper trouble with the director. Not that her paternity claims were exactly newsworthy, but he didn't want to see his and Jenna's names and photos splashed in a newspaper.

"Well?" Cal prompted when Helena continued to look around and didn't say anything else.

"Where do I start?" She seemed to be waiting for an invitation to sit down, but Cal didn't offer. Helena sighed. "My brother is determined to carry out Paul's wishes. They've been friends since childhood when our parents moved to Monte de Leon to start businesses there. Holden was devastated when Paul was killed."

Cal shrugged. "Paul isn't the father of Jenna's child, so there's no wish to carry out."

The last word had hardly left his mouth when he heard a soft whimpering cry sound coming from the nursery.

"Sophie," Jenna mumbled.

"Go to her," Cal advised. "I'll finish up here."

Jenna hesitated. But not for long—the baby's cries were getting louder.

"I do need to talk to Jenna," Helena continued. She opened her purse and rummaged through it. "Do you have a pen? I want to leave my cell number so she can contact me."

That was actually a good idea. He might be able to get approval to trace Helena's calls and obtain a record of her past ones.

Cal didn't have a pen with him, and he looked around before spotting one and a notepad on the kitchen countertop. He got it and glanced into the nursery while he was on that side of the room. Jenna was leaning over the crib changing Sophie's diaper.

"Someone was following Jenna." Cal walked back to Helena and handed her the pen and notepad.

She dodged his gaze, took the pen and wrote down her number. "You mean that reporter across the street? She approached us when we drove up and said she was doing an article about Paul. She said she recognized Holden from newspaper pictures."

Cal shook his head. "Not her. Someone else. A man." He watched for a reaction.

Helena shrugged and handed him the notepad. "You think I know something about it?"

"Do you? The man's name is Anthony Salazar."

Her eyes widened. "Salazar," she repeated on a rise of breath. "You've seen him here in Willow Ridge?"

"I've seen him," Cal confirmed. "Now, mind telling me how you know him?"

Her breath became even more rapid, and she glanced around to make sure it was safe to talk. "Anthony Salazar is evil," she said in a whisper.

He caught her arm when she turned to leave. "And you know this how?"

She opened her mouth but stopped. "Are you wearing a wire?" she demanded.

"No, and I'm not going to strip down to prove it. But you *are* going to give me answers."

Her chin came up. Since he had hold of her arm, he could feel that she was trembling. "You're trying to make me say something incriminating."

Yeah. But for now, Cal would settle for the truth. "What's your connection to Salazar? Does he work for your brother? For you?"

She reached behind her and opened the door. "He worked for Paul."

He hadn't expected that answer. "Paul's dead."

"But his estate isn't."

"What does that mean?" Cal asked cautiously.

"Yesterday was the first anniversary of Paul's death. Early this morning his attorney delivered e-mails of instruction to people named in his will. I saw the list. Salazar got one."

Cal paused a moment to give that some thought. "Are you saying Paul reached out from the grave and hired this man to do something to Jenna?"

"That's exactly what I'm saying." Helena turned and delivered the rest from over her shoulder as she started down the steps. "Neither Holden nor I can call off Salazar. No one can."

Chapter Five

After Jenna changed Sophie's diaper, she gently rocked her until her daughter's whimpers and cries faded. It took just a few seconds before her baby was calm, cooing and smiling at her. It was like magic, and even though it warmed her heart to see her baby so happy, Jenna only wished she could be soothed so easily.

Not much of a chance of that with Holden, his sister and that assassin lurking around. She kept mumbling the poem *"The Raven,"* and hoped the mechanical exercise would keep her calm.

She heard Cal shut and lock the door, and Jenna wanted to be out there while he was talking to Helena. After all, this was her fight, not Cal's. But she also didn't want Holden or Helena anywhere near her baby.

With Helena gone, Jenna went into the

kitchen so she could fix Sophie a bottle. Cal glanced at her, but he had his phone already pressed to his ear, so he didn't say anything to her.

"Hollywood, I need a big favor," Cal said to the person on the other end of the phone line. "The subjects are Holden Carr, Jenna Laniere and Anthony Salazar." He paused. "Yes, the Holden and Jenna from Monte de Leon. I need to know how he found out where she's living. Look for wiretaps first and then dig into her employees. I want to know about any connection with anyone who could have given him this info or photos of Jenna Laniere's baby."

Well, that was a start. Hopefully Cal's contacts would give them an answer soon. It wouldn't, however, solve her problem with Salazar.

She and Sophie needed protection.

And she needed to clear up the paternity issue with Cal's director. And amid all that, she had to make arrangements to move. The apartment was no longer safe now that Holden and Helena Carr knew where she was. Packing wouldn't take long—for the past year, she'd literally been living out of a suitcase, anyway.

With Sophie nestled in the crook of her

arm, Jenna warmed the formula, tested a drop on her wrist to make sure it wasn't too hot, and carried both baby and bottle to the sofa so she could feed her. Sophie wasn't smiling any longer. She was hungry and was making more of those whimpering demands. Jenna kissed her cheek and started to feed her.

Once it was quiet, it was impossible to shut out what Cal was saying. He was still giving someone instructions about checking on the reporter and where to look for Holden Carr's leak, and Cal wanted the person to learn more about some e-mails that might have recently been sent out by Paul's attorney.

She didn't know anything about e-mails, but a leak in communication could mean someone might have betrayed her. There was just one problem with that. Before the trip to the pediatrician, no one including her own household staff and employees had known where she was.

Now everyone seemed to know.

Cal ended his call and scrubbed his hand over his face. He was obviously frustrated. So was Jenna. But she had to figure out a way to get Cal out of the picture. He didn't deserve this, and once she was at a safe location, she could get the DNA test for Sophie.

"So, this is Sophie," he commented,

walking closer. "She's so little for someone who's caused a lot of big waves."

"I'm the one who caused the waves," Jenna corrected.

Cal shrugged it off, but she doubted he was doing that on the inside. "She seems to like that bottle."

"I couldn't breast-feed her. I got mastitis—that's an infection—right after she was born. By the time it'd run its course and I was off the antibiotics, Sophie decided the bottle was for her." Jenna cringed a little, wondering why she'd shared something so personal with a man who was doing everything he could to get her out of his life.

Cal walked even closer, and Sophie responded to the sound of his footsteps by turning her head in his direction. She tracked him with her wide blue-green eyes and fastened her gaze on him when he sat on the sofa next to them. Even with the bottle in her mouth, she smiled at him.

Much to Jenna's surprise, Cal smiled back.

It was a great smile, too, and made him look even hotter than he already was. That smile was a lethal weapon in his arsenal.

"She looks like you," Cal said. "Your face. Your eyes."

"Paul's coloring, though," she added softly. "But when I look at her, I don't see him. I never have. I loved her unconditionally from the first moment I realized I was pregnant." Sheez. More personal stuff.

Why couldn't she stop babbling?

"Helena left you her cell number," Cal said, dropping the notepad onto the coffee table, switching the subject. "She said you're to call her."

Jenna glanced at it and noticed that it had a local area code. "What does she want?"

"Honestly? I don't know. All I know is I don't trust her or Holden." Sophie kicked at him, and he brushed his fingers over her bare toes. He smiled again. But the smile quickly faded. "Helena said that early this morning Salazar received an e-mail from Paul's estate. It might have something to do with why he's here."

Paul again. "It doesn't matter why he's here. I plan to call the Willow Ridge sheriff and see if he can arrest him."

"That's one option. Probably not a good one, though. Salazar won't be easy to catch."

"But we both saw him, right there on Main Street," Jenna pointed out.

Cal nodded. "Unless the local sheriff is

very good at what he does, and very lucky, he could get killed attempting to arrest a man like Salazar."

Oh, mercy. She hadn't even considered that. "Then I have to move sooner than I thought. As soon as Sophie's finished with her bottle, I'll—"

But she stopped there because it involved too many steps and a lot of phone calls.

Where should she start?

"We'll have some information about Holden soon," Cal finished for her. "Once we have that, we'll go from there. It's best if we arrange for someone else to pick up Salazar, not the local sheriff."

"We?" she challenged, wondering why he wasn't excusing himself from this situation.

He kept his attention on Sophie and reached out and touched one of her dark brown curls. "We, as in someone assigned from the International Security Agency."

But not him. A coworker, maybe.

Jenna thought about that for a moment and wondered about the man sitting next to her. She hadn't forgotten the way he'd bashed through a window to save her. "Are you a spy?"

He didn't blink, didn't react. "I'm an operative."

"Is that another word for a spy?"

"It can be." Still no reaction. "The ISA is a sister organization to the CIA. We have no jurisdiction on American soil. We operate only in foreign countries to protect American interests, mainly through rescues and extractions in hostile situations." He took his eyes off Sophie and aimed them at her. "I'm not sure how much I can get involved in your situation."

"I understand." Sophie was finished with her bottle, and Jenna put her against her shoulder so she could burp her. "Besides, I've caused you enough trouble."

He didn't disagree. But there was some kind of debate stirring inside him. "I hadn't expected to want to protect you," he admitted.

Oh. She was surprised not just by his desire to help her, but also by the admission itself. "Why?"

"Why?" he repeated.

She searched his eyes, looking for an answer. Or at least a way to rephrase the question so that it didn't imply the attraction she felt for him. An attraction he probably didn't feel.

"Why did you call my office in Houston last month?" It was something Jenna had wanted to ask since she'd received the message.

Cal shrugged. "The ISA was reopening the investigation into Paul's business dealings and murder. I wanted to make sure you were okay."

"And that's all?" She nearly waved that off. But something in his eyes had her holding her tongue. She wanted to know the reason.

He didn't dodge her gaze. "I was going to see if you'd gotten over Paul. I'd planned to ask you out."

Jenna went still. So maybe the attraction was mutual after all.

She doubted that was a good thing.

"I was over Paul the moment he slapped me for refusing his marriage proposal," Jenna let him know.

His jaw muscles went to war again. "I heard that slap. I was monitoring you with long-distance eavesdropping equipment."

She felt her cheeks flush. It embarrassed her to know that anyone, especially Cal, had witnessed that. The whole incident with Paul was a testament to her poor judgment.

"I've been a screwup most of my life," she admitted.

He made a throaty sound of surprise. "You think that slap was your fault?"

"I think being at Paul's estate was my first mistake. I should have had him investigated before I went down there. I shouldn't have trusted him."

He leaned closer. "Is this where I should remind you about hindsight and that Paul was a really good con artist?"

"It wouldn't help. I've been duped by two other losers. One in college—my supposed boyfriend stole my credit cards and some jewelry. And then there was the assistant I hired right before this mess with Paul. He sold business secrets to my competition." She paused, brought her eyes back to his. "That's why I'm not jumping for joy that you wanted to ask me out."

Cal flexed his eyebrows. "You think I'm a loser like those other guys?"

"No." Shocked that he'd even suggest it, she repeated her denial. "I know you're not. But I have this trust issue now. On top of the damage I've caused your career, I know I'd be bad for you."

He didn't say a word, and the silence closed in around them. Seconds passed.

"Remember when you were lying beneath me in that cantina?" he asked.

"Oh, yes." She winced because she said it so quickly. And so fondly.

"Well, I remember it, too. Heck, I fantasize

about it. I was hoping once I saw you, once I got out my anger over the lie you told, that the fantasies would stop."

Oh, my. Fantasies? This wasn't good. She'd had her own share of fantasies about Cal. Thankfully, she didn't say or do anything stupid. Then Sophie burped loudly, and spit up. It landed on Jenna's shoulder and the front of her sweater.

The corner of Cal's mouth lifted. There was relief in his expression, and Jenna thought he was already regretting this frank conversation.

She glanced down at Sophie, who was smiling now. Jenna wiped her mouth, kissed her on the forehead, put her in the infant carrier seat on the coffee table and buckled the safety strap so that she couldn't wiggle out.

"Could you watch her a minute while I change my top?" Jenna asked.

"Sure." But he didn't look so sure. It was the first time he'd ever seemed nervous. Including when he'd faced gunfire during her rescue.

Jenna stood. So did Cal, though he did keep his hand on the top edge of the carrier. "Forget about that fantasy stuff," he said.

"I will," she lied. "I don't want to cause any more problems for you."

But she had already caused more problems. Jenna could feel it. The attraction was stirring between them. It was a full-fledged tug deep within her belly. A tug that reminded her that despite being a mom, she was still very much a woman standing too close to a too-attractive man.

She fluttered her fingers toward the nursery. "I won't be long." But even with that declaration, she gave in to that tug and hesitated a moment.

Cal cursed softly under his breath. "We'll talk about security plans after you've changed your top."

That should have knocked her back to reality. But while his mouth was saying those practical words, his eyes seemed to be saying, *I want to kiss you.*

Maybe that was wishful thinking.

Either way, Jenna turned before she said something they'd both regret.

She hurriedly grabbed another sweater from the suitcase in the nursery. She shut the door enough to give herself some privacy, but kept it ajar so she could hear if Sophie started to cry. Jenna peeked out to see Cal playing with her daughter's toes while he made some funny faces. The interaction didn't last long—Cal's phone rang, and he answered it.

"Hollywood," Cal greeted. "I hope you have good news for me."

So did Jenna. They desperately needed something to go their way.

She peeled off the soiled sweater, stuffed it into a plastic bag and put it in the suitcase. It would save her from having to pack it in the next hour or two. Then she put on a dark green top and grabbed some other items from around the room to pack those as well.

When she'd finished cramming as much in the suitcase as she could, she took a moment to compose herself. And hated that she didn't feel stronger. But then, it was hard to feel strong when her past relationship with Paul might endanger her daughter.

She peeked out to make sure Sophie was okay. She was. So Jenna waited, listening to Cal's conversation. It was mostly one-sided. He grunted a few responses, and started to curse, but he bit it off when he looked down at Sophie. The profanity and his expression said it all.

"Bad news?" Jenna asked the moment he hung up.

"Some." He looked at Sophie and then glanced around the room. "It's best if you stay put while arrangements are being made for you and Sophie to move."

She walked back to the sofa and sat down across from her daughter. Just seeing that tiny face was a reminder that the stakes were massive now. "Staying put will be safe?"

Cal nodded. "As safe as I can make it."

"You?" she questioned. Not we. "Your director approves of this."

"He approves."

Which meant the situation was dangerous enough for the director to break protocol by allowing her to be guarded by Cal despite the inappropriate conduct that he believed had happened between them.

"How bad is the bad news?" she asked.

He pulled in his breath and walked closer. "Our communications specialist is a guy we call Hollywood. He's very good at what he does, and he can't find an obvious leak, so we don't know how Holden located you. Not yet, anyway. But we were able to get more information about the e-mails sent out by Paul's attorney. Each one was sent from a different account, and one went to your office in Houston. Holden, Helena and Anthony Salazar each got one. The final one went to your reporter friend, Gwen Mitchell."

Gwen Mitchell? So Paul had known her. Funny, the woman hadn't mentioned that particular detail when she'd introduced herself at the grocery store.

Jenna reached for the phone. "Well, my e-mail didn't come to my private or business addresses. I check those several times a day. I'll call my office and see if it arrived in one of the other accounts."

Cal caught her arm to stop her. "The ISA has already retrieved it and taken it off your server. It's encrypted so we'll need the communications guys to take a look at it."

That sounded a bit ominous, so she settled for nodding. "What's in these e-mails?"

"We've only gained access to yours and Salazar's. His e-mail was encrypted as well, but we decided to focus on it first. The encryption wasn't complex, and the computer broke the code within seconds. We're not sure if all the e-mails are similar, but this one appears to be instructions that Paul left with his attorney shortly before his death."

"Instructions?" The content of that e-mail was obviously the bad news that had etched Cal's face with worry. "Paul gave Salazar orders to kill me?"

"Not exactly."

His hesitation caused her heart rate to spike. "Then what?" she asked, holding her breath.

"We're piecing this together using some files we confiscated from Paul's estate and the e-mail sent to Salazar. Apparently before you rejected Paul's proposal and he decided to kill you, he tried to get you pregnant."

Oh, mercy. She'd known Paul was a snake, but she hadn't realized just how far he'd gone with his sinister plan.

"Paul used personal information he got from your corrupt assistant, the one who sold your business secrets," Cal continued. "With some of that information, Paul invited you to his estate when he estimated that you'd be ovulating. He drugged you. That's why you don't remember having sex with him."

She groaned. This just kept getting worse and worse. Everything about their relationship had been a cleverly planned sham. "Paul ditched the plan after I said there was no way I'd marry him."

Cal shrugged. "He intended to kill you, but he also planned for your refusal and your escape."

Jenna felt her eyes widen. "He knew I might escape?"

"Yeah." He let that hang in the air for

several seconds. "He also took into account that he might have succeeded in getting you pregnant. In his e-mail to Salazar, Paul instructed the man to tie up loose ends, depending on how your situation had turned out."

"So, what exactly is Salazar supposed to do?" Jenna didn't even try to brace herself.

Cal glanced at Sophie. Then stared at her. "In the event that you've had a child, which you obviously have, Salazar has orders to kidnap the baby."

Chapter Six

Cal waited for a call while Jenna bathed Sophie. Jenna was smiling and singing to the baby, but he knew beneath that smile, she was terrified.

A professional assassin wanted to kidnap her baby and do God knows what to both her and Sophie in the process. They'd dodged a bullet—Salazar had indeed followed Jenna to the grocery store and hadn't just headed for the apartment to grab Sophie. Maybe he hadn't had the address of the apartment. Or perhaps he wanted to get Jenna first. Maybe he thought if he eliminated the mother, then it'd be a snap to kidnap the child.

That plan left Jenna in a very bad place. She couldn't go on the run, though every instinct in her body was shouting for her to do just that. Running was what Salazar hoped she would do.

She'd be an easy catch.

Cal didn't intend to let that happen. Correction. He had to arrange for someone else to make sure that didn't happen. For the sake of his career, he was going to take these initial steps to keep Sophie and Jenna safe, and then he was going to extract himself from the picture.

He checked his phone to make sure it wasn't dead. It wasn't. And there was still no call from headquarters or Hollywood, who was on the way with some much needed equipment. Cal needed some answers. They were seriously short on those.

Sophie made an "ohhh" sound and splashed her feet and hands in the shallow water that was dabbed with iridescent bubbles. Cal glanced at her to make sure all was okay, and then turned his attention back to the phone.

"Ever heard the expression a watched pot doesn't boil?" Jenna commented. "It's the same with a cell phone. It'll never ring when you're sitting there holding it."

She lifted Sophie from the little plastic yellow tub that Jenna had positioned on the sole bit of kitchen counter space, and she immediately wrapped the dripping wet baby in a thick pink terry-cloth towel.

Cal stood from the small kitchen table and slipped his phone into his pocket in case Jenna needed a hand. But she seemed to have the situation under control. She stood there by the sink, drying Sophie and imitating the soft baby sounds her daughter was making.

He went closer to see the baby's expression. Yep, she was grinning a big gummy grin. Her face was rosy and warm from the bath, and she smelled like baby shampoo. Cal had never thought a happy, freshly bathed baby could grab his complete attention, but this little girl certainly did.

Deep down, he felt something. A strange sense of what it would actually be like to be her father. It would be pretty amazing to hold her and feel her unconditional love.

When he came out of his daddy trance, he realized Jenna was looking at him. Her right eyebrow was slightly lifted. A question: what was he thinking? Cal had no intention of sharing that with her.

"Want to hold her while I get her diaper and gown?" Jenna asked.

Cal felt like someone had just offered to hand him a live grenade. "Uh, I don't want to hurt her."

Jenna smiled and eased Sophie into his

arms. He looked at Jenna. Then Sophie, who was looking at him with suddenly suspicious eyes. For a moment, he thought the baby was going to burst into tears. She didn't, though he wouldn't have blamed her. Instead, she opened her tiny mouth and laughed.

Cal didn't know who was more stunned, Jenna, him or Sophie. Sophie jumped as if she'd scared herself with the unexpected noise from her own mouth. She did more staring, and then laughed again.

"This is a first," Jenna said, totally in awe. Cal knew how she felt. It was like witnessing a little miracle. "I'll have to put it in her baby book." She disappeared into the bedroom-nursery for a moment and came back with Sophie's clothes. "First time you've ever held a baby?" she asked.

He nodded. "My brother, Joe, has a little boy, Austin. He's nearly two years old, but I was away on assignment when he was born. I didn't see him until he was already walking."

"You missed the first laugh, then." She took Sophie from him and went to the sofa so she could sit and dress the baby. "You're close to your family?"

"Yes. No," he corrected. "I mean, we keep in touch, but we're all wrapped up in our jobs. Joe's a San Antonio cop. My other brother is special ops in the military. I started out in the military but switched to ISA."

Jenna had her attention fastened on diapering Sophie and putting on her gown, but Cal knew where her attention really was when he noticed she was trembling. He caught her hand to steady it and helped her pull the gown's drawstring so that Sophie's feet wouldn't be exposed. Sophie didn't seem to mind. The bath had relaxed her, and it seemed as if she was ready to fall asleep.

"Why is Paul sending Salazar after us now?" Jenna asked. She stood and started toward the nursery. "Why wait a year?"

Cal tried not to react to the emotion and fear in her voice. "Could be several reasons," he whispered as he followed her. "Maybe it took this long for his will to get through probate. The courts don't move quickly in Monte de Leon. Or maybe he figured the e-mails would cause a big splash, something to make sure everyone remembers him on the first anniversary of his murder."

"Oh, I remember him." She eased Sophie into the crib, placing the baby on her side, and then after kissing her cheek, Jenna covered her lower body with a blanket. "I didn't need the e-mails or Salazar to do that."

She kissed Sophie again and walked just outside the door, and leaned against the door frame.

A thin breath caused her mouth to shudder.

There was no way he could not react to that. Jenna was hurting and terrified for her daughter. Cal was worried for her, too. The ISA might not be able to stop Salazar before he tried to kidnap Sophie.

Since Jenna looked as if she needed a hug, Cal reached out, slid his arm around her waist and pulled her to him. She didn't resist. She went straight into his arms.

She was soft. *Very* soft. And it seemed as if she could melt right into him. Cal felt his hand move across her back, and he drew her even closer.

Her scent was suddenly on him. A strange mix of baby soap and her own naturally feminine smell. Something alluring. Definitely hot. As was her body. He'd never been much of a breast man, but hers were giving him ideas about how those bare breasts would respond to his touch.

"This isn't a good idea," she mumbled.

Cal knew exactly what she meant. Close

contact wasn't going to cool the attraction. It would fuel it.

But it felt right soothing her on a purely physical level. When he was done here, after Jenna and Sophie were no longer in danger, he needed to spend some time getting a personal life.

He needed to get laid.

Too often he put the job ahead of his needs. Jenna had a bad way of reminding him that the particular activity shouldn't be put off.

She pulled back and met his gaze. The new position put their mouths too close. All he had to do was lean down and press his lips to hers, and Cal was certain the result would be a mind-blowing kiss that neither of them would ever forget.

Which was exactly why it couldn't happen.

Still, that didn't stop his body from reacting in the most basic male way.

With their eyes locked, Jenna put her hand on his chest to push him away. Her middle brushed against his. She froze for a split second, and then went all soft and dewy again. He saw her pupils pinpoint. Felt her warm breath ease from her slightly open mouth. Her pulse jumped on her throat.

She was reacting to his arousal. Her body

was preparing itself for something that couldn't happen.

"I'm flattered," she said, her voice like a silky caress on his neck and mouth.

Uh-oh. She probably meant it to be a joke, a way of breaking the tension. But it didn't break anything. That breath of hers felt like the start of very long French kiss. A kiss he had to nix. He didn't have the time or inclination to deal with a complicated relationship.

Besides, she wasn't his type.

He didn't want a woman that was fragile, so prissy. No, he wanted a woman like him, who liked sex a little rough and with no strings attached. A relationship with Jenna would come with strings longer than the Rio Grande. And he couldn't see her having down-and-dirty sex with him whenever the urge hit.

Her breath brushed against his mouth again, and Cal nearly lost the argument he was having with himself. Knowing he had to do something, fast, he stepped away from her.

In the same instant, there was a knock at the door.

His body immediately went into combat mode, and he drew his gun from his shoulder holster.

"It's me, Hollywood," their visitor called out.

He pushed aside the jolt of adrenaline. "He works for the ISA," Cal clarified to Jenna.

However, he didn't reholster his weapon until he looked out the side window to verify that it was indeed his coworker and that Hollywood wasn't being held at gunpoint. But the man was alone.

Cal opened the door and greeted him. "Thanks for coming." He checked the area in front of the bookstore but didn't see Gwen, the reporter, or either of the Carrs.

"No problem." Hollywood stepped inside and handed Cal a black leather equipment bag. "I brought a secure laptop, a portable security system, an extra weapon and some clothes. I didn't know how long you'd be here so I added some toiletries and stuff."

"Good." Cal didn't know how long he'd be there, either. "Has anyone picked up Salazar?"

"Not yet. We're still looking." Hollywood's attention went in Jenna's direction, and with his hand extended in a friendly gesture, he walked toward her. "Mark Lynch," he introduced himself. "But feel free to call me Hollywood. Everyone does."

"Hollywood," she repeated. She sounded friendly enough, but she was keeping her nerves right beneath the surface.

Cal hoped to do something to help with those nerves, something that didn't involve kissing, so he took out the laptop and turned it on. They needed information, and he would start by reviewing the message traffic on Salazar to see if anyone had spotted him nearby. By now, Salazar knew who Cal was. He would know that the ISA was involved. However, Cal seriously doubted that would send the man running. Salazar wasn't the type.

"We're working on trying to contain Anthony Salazar," Cal heard Hollywood tell Jenna.

"And I'm to stay put until that happens?" she spelled out. She shoved her hand into the back pockets of her pants.

Cal frowned and wondered why he suddenly thought he knew her so well. Jenna and he were practically strangers.

Hollywood glanced at him first and then nodded in response to Jenna's question. "The local sheriff has been alerted to the situation, and the FBI is sending two agents to patrol through the town. Cal can keep things under control here until we can make other arrangements." He took out a folder from the bag and handed it to Cal.

Cal opened it and inside was a woman's

picture. "Kinley Ford?" he read aloud from the background investigation sheet that he took from the envelope. He glanced through the info but didn't recognize anything about the research engineer.

"That file is a little multitasking," Hollywood explained. "The FBI sent her info and picture over this afternoon. She's not associated with Jenna or Salazar, but she's supposedly here in town. She disappeared from Witness Protection, and there are lot of people who want to find her."

Cal shook his head. "Please don't tell me I'm supposed to look for her."

"No. But if anyone asks, that's why you're here. It's the way the director is keeping this all legitimate. He can tell the FBI that you're here in Willow Ridge to try to locate Kinley Ford, as a favor for a sister agency. Don't worry. I'll be the one looking for the missing woman, but your name will be on the paperwork."

Cal breathed a little easier. He wanted to focus on Jenna and Sophie right now.

"I'll set up this temporary security system," Hollywood continued. "And then I'll get out of here so I can stand guard until the FBI agents arrive."

Cal approved of that. The local sheriff would

need help with Salazar around. "What about the background check on Gwen Mitchell?"

"Still in progress, but Director Kowalski found some flags. According to her passport, she was in Monte de Leon during Jenna's rescue."

That grabbed Cal's attention. "Interesting."

"Maybe. But it could mean nothing. She is a reporter, after all. There's nothing to link Gwen to Paul or the Carrs. She appears to have been doing a story on one of the rebel factions."

"And she got out alive." That in itself was a small miracle. Unless Gwen had had a lot of help. The ISA hadn't rescued her, that was for sure, so she must have had other resources to get her out of the country.

"We'll keep digging," Hollywood explained. His voice was a little strained as if he was tired. He rummaged through the bag and came up with several pieces of equipment. "Are these the only windows?" he asked, tipping his head to the trio in the main living area.

"There's a small one in the bathroom," Jenna let him know.

Hollywood nodded and went in that direction to get started. Cal was familiar with the system Hollywood was using. It would arm all entrances and exits so that no one could break in undetected, but it could also be used to create perimeter security to make sure Salazar didn't get close enough to set some kind of explosive or fire to flush them out.

Once the laptop had booted up, Cal logged in with his security code and began to scan through the messages. One practically jumped out at him.

"Here's the e-mail that Paul sent you," Cal told her. "ISA retrieved it and kept it in our classified In-box so I could look at it."

She took a step toward him, but then turned and checked on the baby first. "Sophie's sleeping," Jenna let him know, as she hurried to the sofa to sit beside him.

Cal was positive this e-mail was going to upset her, but he was also positive that they needed to read it. Besides, there might be clues in it that only she would understand, and they might finally make some sense of all of this.

"Jenna, if you've received this e-mail, then I must be dead," she read aloud. *"I doubt my demise has caused you much grief, but it should. Once I have a plan, I don't give up on it. Ever. Our heir will inherit your vast wealth and mine, and will continue what I've started here in Monte de Leon. What the plan doesn't include is you, my dear."*

She stopped, took a deep breath and continued. *"So put your affairs in order, Jenna. I'll be the first person to greet you in the hereafter. See you in a day or two. Love, Paul."*

There were probably several Justice Department and ISA agents already examining the e-mail, but it appeared to be pretty straightforward. A death threat, one that Salazar had probably been paid to carry out.

She groaned softly. "Paul planned for all possibilities. Like a baby. I'm sure the e-mail would have been different if I hadn't had a child." Jenna scrubbed her hands over her face. "And when I woke up this morning, I thought my biggest threat was Holden Carr."

Maybe he still was. Cal was eager to get a look at those other e-mails. All he needed was some kind of evidence or connection that could prompt the FBI to arrest Holden or his sister.

Cal glanced at the notepad on the coffee table. Helena's number was there, and she'd wanted Jenna to call her. While it wouldn't be a pleasant conversation, it might be a necessary one.

Jenna must have followed his gaze. She reached for the notepad and retrieved her cell phone from her purse on the table next to the front door. But before she could press in the numbers, Hollywood came back into the room.

"All secure back there," he informed them. He went to the windows at the front of the apartment and connected a small sensor to each. He put the control monitor on the kitchen table and checked his watch. "I'll be parked on the street near here until I get the okay from the FBI."

Cal stood and went to him to shake his hand. "Thanks, for everything."

"Like I said, no problem. If you need anything else, just give me a call."

Cal let Hollywood out, then closed and locked the door. While he set the security monitor to arm it, Jenna sat on the sofa, dialed the call to Helena and put her cell on speaker.

The woman answered on the first ring. "Jenna," Helena said, obviously seeing the name on her caller ID. Cal made a note to switch Jenna to a prepaid phone that couldn't be traced.

"Why did you want to talk to me?" Jenna immediately asked.

Helena's answer wasn't quite so hasty. She paused for several long moments. "Is your friend, Cal, still there with you?"

"He's here," Cal answered for himself.

It was a gamble. Helena might not say anything important with him listening. But he also didn't want Helena to think that Jenna was alone. That might prompt her to send in Salazar for Sophie—if the man was actually working for Helena, that is. But perhaps the most obvious solution was true—that Salazar was being paid by Paul's estate.

Helena paused again, longer than the first time. "Why didn't you tell us you're an American operative?"

Cal groaned softly. She shouldn't have been able to retrieve that information this quickly. "Who said I am?"

"Sources. *Reliable* ones."

"There are no reliable sources for information like that," Cal informed her. She or Holden had paid someone off. Or else there was a major leak somewhere in the ISA.

"What did you want to talk to me about?" Jenna prompted after a third round of silence.

"Holden," Helena readily answered. "The Justice Department and the ISA have contacted me. They want me to give them evidence so they can arrest my brother for illegal business practices and for Paul's murder."

Jenna glanced at him before she continued. "Is there evidence?"

"For his business dealings. Holden isn't a saint. But there couldn't be evidence for Paul's murder. The housekeeper's responsible for that."

Ah, yes. That mysterious housekeeper again. Cal had monitored Paul's estate for the entire two days of Jenna's visit, and while he'd heard the voices of many of Paul's employees, he hadn't heard of this housekeeper named Mary. Not until after Paul's body had been found with a single execution-style gunshot wound to the head. It'd been the local authorities who'd pointed the finger at the housekeeper, and they had based that on the notes they'd found on Paul's computer. He'd apparently been suspicious of the woman and had decided to fire her. But those notes had been made weeks before his death.

"Did you agree to help the Justice Department and the ISA?" Cal asked, though he was certain he knew the answer.

But he was wrong.

"Yes. I intend to help the authorities bring down my brother," Helena announced.

Jenna's eyes widened, but Cal figured his expression was more of skepticism than surprise. "Are you doing that to get Holden out of the way so you can inherit both Paul's and his estates?"

"No." She was adamant about it. That didn't mean she was telling the truth. "I want the illegal activity to stop. I want the family business to return to the way it was when my parents were still alive."

"Admirable," Cal mumbled. He didn't believe that, either, though he had to admit that it was possible Helena was a do-gooder. But he wasn't about to stake Jenna's and Sophie's safety on that.

"What was in Paul's e-mail to you?" Jenna asked the woman. Cal moved closer to the phone and grabbed the notepad so he could write down the message verbatim.

"The e-mail was personal," Helena explained. "Though I'm sure it won't stay that way long. Cal will see to that."

Yes, he would. "If that's true, then you might as well tell me what it says."

This was the longest silence of all. "Paul said he would see me in the hereafter in a day or two."

Almost identical wording to Jenna's e-mail, but Cal jotted it down anyway. "Why would Paul want you dead?"

"I don't know." Helena sighed heavily, and

it sounded as if she had started to cry. "But he obviously believes I wronged him in some way. Maybe Paul wanted Holden to inherit everything, and this is his way of cutting me out of his estate."

Or maybe Holden had gotten a death threat, too. But then with plans to have Sophie kidnapped, that left Cal with a critical question. Whom had Paul arranged to raise the child? Certainly not an assassin like Salazar.

He thought about that a moment and came full circle to the fifth recipient of one of Paul's infamous e-mails.

Gwen Mitchell.

He needed a full background report on her ASAP. It was possible that she was connected to Paul.

"Jenna, we're both in danger," Helena continued. "That's why we have to work together to stop this person that Paul has unleashed on us."

"Work together, how?" Jenna asked.

"Meet with me tomorrow morning. Alone. No Holden and no Cal Rico."

That wasn't going to happen. Still, Cal had to keep this channel of communication open. "Jenna will get back to you on that," he answered.

"Be at the Meadow's Bed-and-Breakfast tomorrow morning at ten," Helena continued as if this meeting was a done deal. "It's a little place in the country, about twenty miles from Willow Ridge. I'll see you then." And with that, she hung up.

Jenna clicked the end-call button. She wasn't trembling like before. Well, not visibly, anyway. "Do you think she wants to kill me, too?"

He considered several answers and decided to go with the truth. "Anything's possible at this point." But he did need to get a look at all the e-mails to get a clearer picture.

"I'm scared for Sophie," she whispered.

Yeah. So was he. And being scared wasn't good. It meant he'd lost his objectivity. He blamed that on holding Sophie. On that first laugh. Oh, and the cuddling session with Jenna. None of those things should have happened, and they'd sucked him right in and gotten him personally involved.

Jenna swiveled around to face him, blinking back tears, and moved closer into his arms.

And Cal let her.

"I'm not a wimp," she declared. "I run a multimillion-dollar business. And if the threats were aimed just at me, I'd be spitting mad. But my baby is in danger."

Cal couldn't refute that. Heck, he couldn't even reassure her that Salazar wouldn't make a full-scale effort to kidnap Sophie. All he could do was sit there and hold Jenna.

A single tear streaked down her cheek, and Cal caught it with his thumb, his fingers cupping her chin. And he was painfully aware that he was using his fingers to lift her chin. Just slightly.

So he could put his mouth on hers.

And that's exactly what he did.

The touch was a jolt that went straight through him like a shot. It didn't help that Jenna made a throaty feminine sound of approval. Or that she slid her arms around his neck and drew him closer.

Cal cursed himself for starting this. And worse, for continuing it and deepening the kiss. French-kissing Jenna was the worst idea he'd ever had, but that jolt of fire that her mouth was creating overruled any common sense he had left. She tasted like silk and sin, and he wanted a whole lot more.

He heard a ringing sound and thought it was another by-product of the jolt. But when the ringing continued, Cal realized passion wasn't responsible. His cell phone was. He untangled himself from Jenna and checked the caller ID screen.

It was Director Kowalski.

"Hell," he mumbled. Cal quickly tried to compose himself before he answered it. "Agent Rico."

"We might have a problem," the director started. That wasn't the greeting Cal wanted to hear. "First of all, I just read the e-mail that Paul Tolivar supposedly sent Jenna. You think it's legit?"

Cal had given that some thought. He should have given it more. "I'm not sure. Anyone close to Paul could have composed those e-mails and sent them out. Anyone with an agenda." He glanced at Jenna. There was no surprise in her eyes, which meant she'd already come up with that theory.

"You have someone in mind?"

This was easy. Cal didn't even have to think about it. "Helena or Holden Carr. Both inherited a lot of money from Paul. Also, those flags on Gwen Mitchell might turn out to be a problem."

"Yes, we're working on her. But something else has popped up." The director took in an audible breath. "We might be wrong, but there are new flags. Ones within the department."

Everything inside Cal went still. This was worse than bad news. "What's wrong?"

"We think we might have a leak in communications who could have been responsible for alerting Gwen Mitchell and the Carrs as to Jenna Laniere's whereabouts."

"A leak might not have been necessary for that. Holden or Helena Carr could have been watching Jenna's estate and then followed her when she went there." Of course, that didn't explain how they'd known about Sophie, unless the person watching the estate had seen the baby in the car. That was possible, but it sounded as if the director thought someone or something else might have been responsible. "Who do these flags point to?"

"Not to anyone specific, but if it's true, the source of the information has to be in ISA."

Oh, man. The bad news just kept getting worse. They might have a traitor within the organization. "Who in ISA would have access to the pool of information that would affect all the players in this case?"

Kowalski blew out an audible breath. "Mark Lynch is a possibility."

That was not the name he'd expected to hear the director say. "Hollywood," Cal mumbled.

"I know he's on the way there with equipment. And I know you two are friends. I didn't learn about the flags until a few minutes ago."

And that in itself could be a problem because it meant someone was trying to cover their tracks. Or else set someone up. "What exactly are these flags?"

"Hollywood monitored the message traffic pertaining to Jenna Laniere. Faxes, e-mails, telephone calls. The info in question went from Paul Tolivar to his lawyer. It was her detailed financial data, including passwords and codes for her business accounts."

Cal knew about those messages that'd been sent a year ago while Jenna was in Monte de Leon. Paul had gotten into Jenna's laptop the first day she was at his estate and had copied her entire hard drive. Though Paul had only sent those messages to his lawyer, it didn't mean that someone else couldn't have learned the contents, saved them and now sent them out again. But why do it now, especially since the information was a year old?

That led Cal to his next question. "Why do you think Hollywood's the one who compromised this information?"

"Because we intercepted an encrypted message that was meant for him. The message was verification of receipt of Ms. Laniere's info and details about the payment for services rendered. We checked, and there has been money sent to an account in the Cayman Islands."

Cal tried not to curse. He didn't want a gut reaction to make him accuse his friend of a crime he might not have committed. "That still doesn't mean Hollywood's guilty. One or both of the Carrs could be trying to set him up to make it look as if he sold Jenna's financial information. And they might be doing that to get us to focus on Hollywood and not them."

"Could be." But the director didn't sound at all convinced of that. "It's a lot of money, Cal. If the Carrs had wanted to set someone up, why wait until now?"

That timeline question kept coming up, and Cal still didn't have an answer for it. Was it tied to Sophie? And if so, how?

"There's a final piece to this mess," the director continued. "We accessed Hollywood's personal computer, and we found several encrypted messages from Anthony Salazar. In the most recent one, Salazar asks Hollywood to help him with the kidnapping."

Cal couldn't fight off the gut reactions any longer. He felt sick to his stomach. Yes, it could all be a setup, but it was a huge risk to take if it wasn't. Hell. Had he been that wrong about a man he considered a friend?

"We tried to stop Hollywood before he left to go see you. But when he gets there, tell him he's to report back to me immediately. Don't let him in," Kowalski warned.

Cal groaned. "He's already been here. He installed the equipment and left."

The director cursed. "He wasn't supposed to be there yet. He had instructions to arrive at 9:00 p.m."

Cal got to his feet and glanced around. At the equipment bag. At the laptop he'd used to read the e-mail Paul sent Jenna. At the security systems that Hollywood had activated a full hour ahead of schedule.

"What are my orders?" Cal asked. He motioned for Jenna to get Sophie.

"We might have a rogue agent on our hands. Get Ms. Laniere and her daughter out of there," the director ordered. *"Now."*

Chapter Seven

The nightmare was back.

This time, she wasn't in Monte de Leon, and there were no rebel soldiers. Jenna knew this was much worse—her precious baby was in danger.

"Bring as little as possible," Cal instructed in a whisper. He stuffed diapers and some of Sophie's clothes into her bag and added a flashlight. "Hurry," he added.

Not that she needed him to remind her of that. Everything about his movements and body language indicated they had to move fast.

"What kind of flags did you say the director found on Hollywood?" Jenna whispered. Cal had told her that Hollywood might have bugged the place. He might be listening to their every word.

"They don't have a full picture yet." Cal looped the now full diaper bag over his shoulder and motioned for her to pick up Sophie. "You'll have to carry her. I need at least one hand free."

So he could shoot his gun if it became necessary.

"Does your car have an infant seat already in it?" he mouthed.

She nodded and scooped the sleeping baby into her arms. Thankfully, Sophie didn't wake up. "I'm parked just behind the bookstore. The keys are in my purse."

Jenna wanted to ask if it was safe to take her car. But maybe it didn't matter. They had to take the risk and get out of there.

Cal drew his gun while she swaddled Sophie in a thick blanket. The moment she finished, she motioned for them to go. He paused a moment at the door. Then he opened it and glanced around outside.

"Let's go," he ordered.

Jenna grabbed her purse. She stuffed her cell phone into it, extracted her keys and stepped out into the cold night air. It was dark, and there was no moon because of the cloudy sky, but the bookstore had floodlights positioned on the four corners of the building.

Cal kept her behind him while they made their way down the stairs. He stopped again and didn't give her the signal to move until he'd glanced around the side of the store. Once he had them moving again, he kept them next to the exterior wall.

It seemed to take a lifetime to walk the twenty yards or so to her car. She unlocked the door with her keypad, but instead of letting her get in, Cal motioned for her to stand back. She did. And he used the flashlight to check the undercarriage for explosives.

God. What a mess they were in.

After Cal had gone around the entire perimeter of the car, he caught onto her and practically shoved them in through the passenger's side. Jenna turned to put Sophie in the rear-facing car seat, but a sound stopped her cold.

Footsteps.

Standing guard in front of her, Cal lifted his gun and took aim.

"Don't shoot," someone whispered. It was a woman's voice, and Jenna expected to see Helena step from the shadows.

Instead, it was Gwen Mitchell.

She lifted her hands in a show of surrender. She didn't appear to be armed and unlike the meeting in the grocery store, the woman didn't have a camera.

"I have to talk to you," Gwen said.

"This isn't a good time for conversation." Cal kept his gun aimed at Gwen, and he shut the car door. However, he didn't leave her side to get in. He stood guard, and Jenna made use of his body shield. She leaned over and put Sophie in the infant seat. She strapped her in and then climbed into the backseat with her in case she had to do what Cal was doing—use her body as a final defense.

"It's important," Gwen added.

Everything was important right now, especially getting out of there. Jenna glanced around and prayed that Salazar wasn't using Gwen as a diversion so he could sneak up on them and try to kidnap Sophie.

"We should go," Jenna reminded Cal.

Gwen fastened her attention on Jenna. "A few minutes ago I sent you a copy of the e-mail that I got from Paul. Read it and you'll know why it's important that we talk. Then get in touch with me."

Jenna hadn't brought her laptop, but she thought maybe her BlackBerry was in her purse. Once they were on the road and away from there, she'd check and see if the e-mail had arrived into her personal account. But for now, she continued to keep watch and wished that she had a weapon to defend Sophie and herself with.

"Keep your hands lifted," Cal instructed Gwen, and he began to inch his way to the driver's side of the car.

"Don't trust anyone," Gwen continued. "There's something going on. I don't know what. But I think Paul's left instructions for someone to play a sick game. I think he wants to pit each of us against the other."

Then Paul had succeeded. Five e-mails. Five people. And there wasn't any trust among them. It was too big of a risk to start trusting now.

"Did he say anything about me in the e-mail he sent to you?" Gwen asked.

"No," Jenna assured her.

"You're sure? Because I'm trying to figure out why he contacted me. Do you have any idea?"

Cal didn't answer. He'd had enough, and got into the car and started the engine. He drove away, fast, leaving Gwen to stand there with her question unanswered.

"The way she said Paul's name makes me think she knew him well," Jenna commented. She kept her eyes on the woman until she was no longer in sight.

"How well she knew him is what I need to find out. Right after I get you and Sophie to someplace safe."

With all the rush to leave her apartment, she hadn't considered where to go. First things first, they had to make sure no one was following them, or there wouldn't be any safe place to escape to.

Cal sped down Main Street. Thankfully, there was no traffic. It wasn't unusual for that time of night—Willow Ridge wasn't exactly a hotbed of activity. He took the first available side road to get them out of there.

Jenna continued to keep watch around them. She wanted to get her BlackBerry, but that could wait until she was sure they weren't in immediate danger. However, maybe she could get some answers to other questions. After all, her baby's life was in danger, and Jenna wanted to know why.

"What made your director think we couldn't trust Hollywood?" she asked.

Like her, Cal was looking all around. "He thinks Hollywood transferred some information he obtained through official message traffic that he was monitoring."

"Information about me?"

"Yeah," he answered as if he was thinking hard about that.

She certainly was. "I met Hollywood for the first time tonight. He doesn't even know me." But that didn't mean he couldn't be working for one of the other players in this. "You don't think Paul got to him, too?"

"I don't know. He was in Monte de Leon during your rescue, and he had access to any and all information flowing in and out of Paul's estate. There are plenty of people who would have paid for that information."

She considered that a moment while she stared back at the dark road behind them. The lights of Willow Ridge were just specks now. "Do you trust Hollywood?"

"Before tonight I thought I did." He shook his head. "But I can't risk being wrong. It's possible he got greedy and decided to sell your financial information to someone. If he's innocent, then what we're doing is just a waste of time."

But it didn't feel like a waste. It felt like a necessity.

"I changed all my passwords and account information after Paul was killed," Jenna explained. "So, unless someone's gotten their hands on the new info, those old codes won't do them any good." Of course, maybe Hollywood didn't know they were old.

"If someone were using this to set him up, it wouldn't matter if the codes were outdated. The unauthorized message traffic is enough to incriminate him."

So Hollywood could be innocent. Still, they were on the run, and that meant someone had succeeded in terrifying her.

"Any idea where we're going?" she asked.

Cal checked his watch and the rearview mirror. "I'm sure the director is making arrangements for a safe house. All previous arrangements will be ditched because Hollywood would have had access to the plans."

"So it could take a while." Jenna believed Cal would do whatever it took to keep Sophie safe, but she wasn't certain that would be enough.

"How far is your estate?" he asked.

She'd hoped there wouldn't be any more surprises tonight. "About two hours." But Jenna shook her head. "You're thinking about going there?"

"Temporarily."

Oh, mercy. She hated to point out the obvious, but she would. "The reason I'm not there now is the threats from Holden."

"Holden might be the least of our worries," Cal mumbled. And she knew it was true. "How good is the estate's security system?"

"It's supposed to be very good." Her surprise was replaced by frustration. "In hindsight, I should have stayed put there, beefed up security and told Holden where he could shove his threats. Then we wouldn't be running for our lives."

Cal met her gaze in the mirror. "You were scared and pregnant. I don't think your decision to leave was based solely on logic."

"Pregnancy hormones," she said under her breath. She couldn't dismiss that they hadn't played a part in her going on the run. But hiding had made her pregnancy more bearable, and it'd saved her from having to explain to her friends that she'd gotten pregnant by an accused felon.

"I've spent a lot of my life running," she commented. Why she told him that she didn't know. But she suddenly felt as if she owed him an explanation as to why she'd left the safety of the estate and headed for a small town where she knew no one. "Before my parents were killed in a car accident, when we'd have an argument, I'd immediately leave and take a long trip somewhere."

He shrugged. "There's nothing wrong with traveling."

"This wasn't traveling. It was escaping." Heck, she was still escaping. And this time, she might not succeed. Sophie might have to pay the ultimate price for Jenna's bad choices. "I have to make this right for Sophie. I can't let her be in danger. She's too important to me."

"I understand," he said. "She's important to me, too."

And for some reason, that wasn't like lip service. He wasn't just trying to console her.

Cal had only known Sophie a few hours. There was no way he could have developed such strong feelings for her. Was there? Maybe the little girl had brought out Cal's paternal instincts. Or maybe he was just protecting them. Either way, it was best not to dwell on it. Once they got to her estate, Cal would leave. After all, he had a career to salvage.

Jenna checked on Sophie again. She was still asleep and would probably stay that way for several hours. With no immediate threat, it was a good time to check for that Black-Berry. Jenna climbed over the seat, buckled up and grabbed the purse that she'd tossed onto the floor.

It took several moments for the Black-Berry to load and for her to scroll through the messages. There was indeed one that Gwen had forwarded to her.

"Gwen, I expect you're surprised to hear from me," Jenna read aloud. *"When I was considering whom to give this particular task, I thought of several candidates, but you're the best woman for the job. Yes, this is a job offer. You see, I've been murdered, and if you're reading this, then my killer is still out there. I want you to use your skills as an investigative journalist and find proof of who that person is. Once you have the proof, contact Mark Lynch at the International Security Agency."*

"Mark?" Cal repeated. "Why would Paul want her to contact Hollywood?"

Jenna exchanged puzzled glances with him. "Obviously, Paul knew him. Or knew *of* him. But why would Paul trust Hollywood with that kind of information? Why not just turn it over to Holden or Salazar?"

Cal didn't say anything for several seconds. "Maybe he's giving each person one task. Or maybe Gwen is right and this is his way of dividing and conquering. If you're all at odds and suspicious of each other, then he'll get some kind of postmortem satisfaction. He sends Salazar after Sophie. Gwen, after the person who murdered him. And he somehow turns Helena against her own brother."

Yes. Jenna would have loved to know what Paul had written to Helena. Or to Holden. If they had all the e-mails, they might be able to figure out what Paul was really trying to do.

"Did you read the entire e-mail?" Cal asked.

"No. There's more." She scrolled down the tiny screen. *"If you find my killer, then my attorney will wire the sum of one million dollars to a bank account of your choice. I'm giving you one week. If you don't have the proof, the job will go to someone else."*

So this wasn't going to stop. If Gwen failed, then the investigation would continue.

"Maybe Hollywood will be offered the job," Cal speculated. "Or Salazar."

She heard him, but her attention was on the last lines of the e-mail. *"To make things easier for you, I want you to focus your efforts on my number-one suspect,"* she continued reading aloud. *"Actually, she's my only suspect. Her name is Jenna Laniere."*

That was it. The end of Paul's instructions.

Jenna had to take a moment to absorb it. "Paul obviously didn't trust me right from the start, or he wouldn't have written this e-mail."

"If he's the one who wrote it."

She turned in the seat to face Cal. "What are you thinking?"

"I'm thinking Gwen, Holden or Helena could be behind these messages from the grave." He hissed out a breath. "Even Holly-wood could have done it. This could all be some kind of ploy to get Paul's estate."

Maybe. After all, Holden and Helena had shared Paul's money. Maybe one of them wanted it all. Or if Gwen was the culprit, maybe this was her way of ferreting out a story.

But how did Hollywood fit into this? Unless the man was just an out-and-out criminal, she couldn't figure out a logical scenario where he'd be collecting any of Paul's money.

"Maybe your friend's innocent," Jenna said, thinking out loud. "What if someone is setting him up so you can't trust him? That way, it would be one less person you could turn to for help."

Cal lifted his shoulder. "It's possible, I suppose. Once the director has gone through all the message traffic, we should know more."

Yes, but would that information stop her daughter from being in danger? Jenna couldn't shake the fear that Sophie was at the core of all of this.

Something caught her eye.

Headlights in the distance behind them.

Cal noticed it, too. His attention went straight to the rearview mirror. Neither of them said anything. They just sat there, breaths held, waiting to see what would happen.

He kept his speed right at fifty-five, and the headlights got closer very quickly. The other car was speeding. Still, that in itself was no cause for alarm. Combined with everything, however, her heart and mind were racing with worst-case scenarios.

"Get in the backseat and stay down," Cal insisted.

Jenna tried to keep herself steady. This could be just a precaution, she reminded herself, but she did as he asked. She climbed onto the seat with Sophie and positioned her torso over the baby so that she could protect her still-sleeping baby. But she also wanted to keep watch, so she craned her neck so she could see the side mirror.

The car was barreling down on them.

Jenna prayed it would just pass them and that would be the end to this particular scare. She could see Cal's right hand through the gap of the seats, and because of the other car's bright headlights, she could also see his finger tense on the trigger of his gun. He had the weapon aimed at the passenger's window.

The lights got even brighter as the car came upon them. Too close. It was a dark SUV, much larger than her own vehicle. Jenna braced herself because it seemed as if the SUV was going to ram right into them.

"Is it Salazar?" she asked in a raw whisper. Her heart was pounding now. Her breath was coming out in short, too-fast jolts.

"I can't tell. Just stay down."

Jenna didn't have a choice. She had to do whatever she could to protect Sophie. As meager as it was, her body would become a shield if the driver of that vehicle started shooting.

The headlights slashed right at the mirror when the car bolted out into the passing lane. She prayed it would continue to accelerate and go past them.

But it didn't.

With her heart in her throat, Jenna watched as the car slowed until it was literally side by side with them. Cal cursed under his breath and aimed his gun.

"Brace yourself," he warned her a split second before he slammed on the brakes.

She saw a flash of red from the other car.

The driver had braked as well, and the lights lit up the darkness, coating their shadows with that eerie shade of bloodred.

Cal threw the car into Reverse and hit the accelerator. She didn't know how he managed, but he spun the car around so they were facing in the opposite direction, and gunned the engine.

There was another flash of brake lights from the SUV. The sound of the tires squealing against the asphalt. Jenna squeezed her eyes shut a moment and prayed. But when she looked into the mirror, her worst fear was confirmed.

The SUV was coming at them again.

If it rammed them or sideswiped them, it'd be difficult for Cal to stay on the road. It was too dark to see if there were ditches nearby or one of the dozens of creeks that dotted the area. But Jenna didn't need to see things like that to know the danger. If the SUV driver managed to get them off the road, he could fire shots at a stationary target. They wouldn't be hard to hit.

"Should I call the sheriff?" she asked. She had to do something. *Anything.*

"He wouldn't get here in time."

The last ominous word had hardly left

Cal's mouth when there was a loud bang. The SUV rammed into the back of her car, and the jolt snapped her body. Jenna caught Sophie's car seat and held on, trying to steady it and brace herself for a second hit.

It came hard and fast.

The front bumper of the SUV slammed into them. The motion jostled Sophie, and she stirred, waking.

"Get all the way down," Cal instructed. "Put your hand over Sophie's ears and cover her as much as you can with the blanket."

She did, though Jenna had to wonder how that would help. A moment later, she got her answer. He didn't slow down. Didn't try to turn around again. He merely turned his gun in the direction of the back window and the SUV. Cal used the rearview mirror to aim.

And he fired.

The blast was deafening. Louder than even the impact of the SUV. That sound rifled through Jenna, spiking her fear and concern for her child. Even though she had clamped her hands around Sophie's ears, the sound got through and her baby shrieked.

Cal fired again and again.

The bullets tore through the back window, the safety glass webbing and cracking, but it stayed in place. Thank God. Even though the glass wasn't much protection, she didn't want it tumbling down on Sophie.

Cal fired one more shot and then jammed his foot on the accelerator to get them out of there.

Chapter Eight

Cal sped through the wrought-iron gates that fronted Jenna's estate.

He'd spent most of the trip watching the road, to make sure that SUV hadn't followed them. As far as he could tell, it hadn't, even though they had encountered more traffic the closer they got to Houston. And then the traffic had trailed off to practically nothing once he was on the highway that led to Jenna's house.

Though the estate was only twenty miles from Houston city limits and there were other homes nearby, it felt isolated because it was centered on ten pristine acres.

The iron gates were massive, at least ten feet tall and double that in width. Fanning off both sides of the gate was a sinister-looking spiked-top fence that appeared to surround the place. Even though there was no guard in the small redbrick gatehouse to the left, the builder had obviously planned for security, which made Cal wonder why Jenna had ever left in the first place. Yes, she'd told him she had a tendency to take off when things got rough, but the estate was as close to a stronghold as they could get. Somehow, he'd have to make Jenna understand that this was their best option. For now. He'd have to try to soothe her flight instinct so she wouldn't be tempted to run.

He stopped in the circular drive directly in front of the house and positioned the car so that Jenna would only be a few steps away from getting inside. He didn't want her exposed any longer than necessary. Salazar had expert shooting skills with a long-range assault rifle.

Like the rest of the property, the house was huge. There was a redbrick exterior and a porch with white columns that stretched across the entire front and sides. The carved oak front door opened, and he immediately reached for his gun.

"It's okay," Jenna assured him. "That's Meggie, the housekeeper. She's worked here since I was a baby."

The woman was in her mid-sixties with graying flame-red hair. Short, but not petite, she wore a simple blue-flowered dress. She didn't rush to greet them, but she did give them a warm smile when Jenna stepped from the car with a sleeping Sophie cradled in her arms.

"Welcome home. I have rooms made up for all of you," Meggie announced. Her words came out in a rushed stream of excitement. "When you called and said you were on the way, I got the crib ready in the nursery. The bedding is already turned down for the little angel. And I put your guest in the room next to yours."

"Thank you," Jenna muttered.

Once they were inside and the door was shut, Meggie patted Jenna's cheek and eased back the blanket a bit so she could see Sophie. She smiled again, and her aged blue eyes went to Cal. "She looks like you."

He wasn't sure what to say to that, so he didn't say anything. Meggie thought Sophie was his.

Cal forced himself to assess his surroundings. He'd expected luxury, and wasn't disappointed. Vaulted ceilings. Marble floors. Victorian antiques. But there were also a lot of windows and God knows how many points of entry. It would be a bear to keep all of them secure.

"We're exhausted," Jenna said to the woman, her voice showing her nerves. Maybe the nerves were from Meggie's comment about Sophie's looks but more likely from the inevitable adrenaline crash. "We'll get settled in for the night and we can talk tomorrow. There are things I should tell you."

Meggie nodded, and lightly kissed Sophie's cheek.

"Where's the main security panel?" he asked before Meggie could walk away.

She pointed to a richly colored oil landscape painting in the wide corridor just off the foyer. "The access code is seven, seven, four, one." Then she made her exit in the opposite direction.

Jenna let out a deep breath. A shaky one. Now that she was safe inside, the impact of what'd happened was hitting her. She was ready to crash, but Cal needed to take a few security measures before he helped her put Sophie to bed.

He aimed for some small talk so he could get some information about the place. And maybe get her mind off the nightmare they'd just come through.

"You were born here?" Cal asked, going to the monitor. The painting had a hinged front, and he opened it so he could take a look at what he had to work with.

"Literally. My mother didn't trust hospitals. So my dad set up one here. In fact, he set up a lot of things here, mainly so that we'd never have to leave."

"They were overly protective?" Cal armed the system and watched as the lights flashed on to indicate the protected areas.

"Yes, with a capital Y. My mother was from a wealthy family, and she'd been kidnapped for ransom when she was a child. Obviously it was a life-altering experience for her. She was obsessed with keeping me safe, and over the years, Dad began to share that obsession. What they failed to remember was that my mother had been kidnapped from her own family's house."

Jenna followed his sweeping gaze around the room before her eyes met his. "There really is no place that's totally safe. Sometimes this estate felt more like a prison than a home."

That explained her wanderlust and maybe even the reason she'd gone to Monte de Leon. For months Cal had seen that trip as a near fatal mistake, but then he glanced at Sophie. That little girl wouldn't be here if Jenna hadn't made that trip. Maybe it was the camaraderie he'd developed with Jenna as they'd waited on that cantina floor. Whatever it was, that bonding had obviously extended to the child in her arms.

"Is the security system okay?" she asked.

"It looks pretty good." The back of the faux painting had the layout of the estate and each room was thankfully labeled not just for function but for the type of security that was installed. "The perimeter of the fence is wired to detect a breach. You have motion detectors at every entrance and exit. And all windows. This is a big place," he added in a mumble.

"Yes," she said with a slight tinge of irony. "Any weak spots you can see?"

"Front gate," he readily supplied. "Is it usually open the way it was when we came in?"

She nodded. "But it can be closed by pressing the button on the monitor or the switch located just inside the grounds." Jenna reached over and did just that. "There's an automatic lock and keypad entry on the left side of the gate."

Which wasn't very safe. Keypads could be tampered with or bypassed. Hollywood certainly knew how to do those things. Salazar likely did, too.

"What's this?" he asked, tapping the large

area on the south side of the house that was labeled Gun Room.

"My father was an antique gun collector. He built an indoor firing range to test guns before he bought them."

Interesting. He hadn't expected that, but he would add it to his security plan. "You can shoot?"

"Not at all. The noise always put me off. But I'm willing to learn. In fact, I want to learn."

He just might teach her. Not so he could use her as backup. But it might make her feel more empowered. Plus, the room might come in handy, because it was almost certainly bullet-proof. If worse came to worst, then he might have to move them in there. For now, though, he looked for a more comfortable solution.

"Where are the rooms we're supposed to stay in?" he asked. When Jenna shifted a little, he realized that Sophie was probably getting heavy. He holstered his gun and gently took the baby from her. The little girl was a heavy sleeper. She didn't even lift an eyelid.

"Thanks." Jenna touched her index finger to a trio of rooms on the east side of the house. "That's the nursery, my room's next to it and that's the guest room."

He put his finger next to hers. Touching

her. She didn't move away. In fact, she slipped her hand over his. It was such a simple gesture. But an intimate one. It was a good thing Sophie was between them, or he might have done something stupid like pull Jenna into his arms.

"There's a problem," he let her know.

The corner of her mouth lifted for just a second. "I think we're too tired to worry about another kissing session."

There was no such thing as being too tired to kiss. But Cal didn't voice that. Instead, he moved his hand away to avoid further temptation. "Your bedroom has exterior doors."

"Two of them. And another door leads to the pool area. The guest room has an exterior door as well."

From a security perspective, that wasn't good. "How about the nursery?"

"No exterior doors. Four windows, though."

He'd take the windows over the doors. "That's where we'll be spending the night."

She didn't question it. Jenna turned and started walking in that direction. Cal followed her, trying to keep his steps light so he wouldn't wake Sophie. Jenna led him down a corridor lined with doors and stopped in front of one.

"Don't turn on the lights," Cal told her when she opened the door. It was possible that Holden or someone else was doing some long-range surveillance, and Cal didn't want to advertise their exact location in the estate.

He took a moment to let his eyes adjust to the darkness, and he saw the white crib placed against an interior wall well away from the windows. That was good. Cal went that direction and eased Sophie onto the mattress. She moved a little and pursed her lips, sucking at a nonexistent bottle, and he braced himself for her to wake up and cry. But her eyes stayed closed.

"There isn't a bed in here," Jenna whispered. "Just that."

He spotted a chaise longue in the small adjacent sitting room just off the nursery. The chaise wasn't big enough for two people, but hopefully it would be comfortable enough for Jenna to get some sleep.

"I can have a bed brought in," she suggested.

"No. Best not to have any unnecessary movement." Nor did he want to alert anyone else in the household to their sleeping arrangements. Tomorrow, they'd work out something more comfortable.

Jenna walked mechanically to a closet and

took out two quilts. The rooms were toasty warm, but she handed him one and draped the other around herself. Since she didn't seem steady on her feet, Cal helped her in the direction of the chaise.

"Get some sleep," he instructed.

She moved as if she were about to climb onto the chaise, but then she stopped. There was just enough moonlight coming through the windows that he could easily see her troubled expression.

"I've really made a mess of things," she said.

Oh, no. Here it was. The adrenaline crash. Reality was setting in, and she started to shake. He couldn't see any tears, but he had no doubt they were there.

She moved again. Closer to him. Until they were touching, her breasts against his chest. That set off Texas-size alarms in his head, and the rest of his body, but it didn't stop him from putting his arms around her.

She sobbed softly, but tried to muffle it by putting her mouth against his shoulder. Her warm breath fluttered against his neck.

"You'll get through this," he promised, though he knew it wouldn't be easy. She was in for a long, hard night. And so was he.

"You're not trembling," she pointed out.

"I'm trained not to tremble. Besides, I only shot an SUV tonight. Trust me, I've done worse." He tried to make it sound light. Cocky, even. But he failed miserably. The attack couldn't be dismissed with bravado.

She pulled back and blinked hard, trying to rid her eyes of the tears. "Have you ever killed anyone?"

Cal was a little taken aback with the question, and he kept his answer simple. "Yeah."

"Good."

"Good?" Again, he was taken aback.

Jenna nodded. "I want you to stop Salazar if he comes after Sophie."

Oh. Now he got it. Cal pushed her hair away from her face. "I won't let him hurt her. Or you."

Hell. He hadn't meant to say that last part aloud. It was too personal, and it was best if he tried to keep some barrier between them.

Her mouth came to his, and all that barrier stuff suddenly sounded like something he didn't want after all. He wanted her kiss.

Since it was going to be a major mistake, Cal decided to make the most of it. Something they'd both regret. And maybe that would stop them from doing it again. So he took far more than he should have.

He hooked his arm around her, just at the top of her butt. He drew her closer so that it wasn't only their chests and mouths that were touching. Their bodies came together, and the fit was even better than his fantasies.

The soft sound Jenna made was from a silky feminine moan of pleasure. A signal that she not only wanted this but wanted more. She wrapped her arms around him and gently ground her sex against his.

While the body contact was mind-blowing, Cal didn't neglect the kiss. This last kiss. Since he'd already decided there couldn't be any more of them, he wanted to savor her in these next few scorching moments. To brand her taste, her touch, the feel of her into his memory.

The kiss was already hot and deep. He deepened it even more. Because he was stupid. And because his stupidity knew no boundaries, he followed Jenna's lead.

Oh, man. Their clothes weren't thick enough. A wall wouldn't have been thick enough.

He could feel the heat of her sex. And his. The brainless part of him was already begging him to lower Jenna to that chaise and strip off her pants. Sex would follow immediately. Great hot sex. Which couldn't happen, of course. Sophie was just in the adjoining room and could wake up at any minute.

Cal repeated that, and he forced himself to stop. When he stepped back from her, both of them were gasping for breath.

"Good night," he managed to say.

"That was your idea of a good-night kiss?" Jenna challenged.

No. It was his idea of foreplay, but it was best not to say that out loud. "We can't do it again."

Why did it sound as if he was trying to convince himself?

Because he was.

Still, he was determined to make this work. He was a pro. A rough-around-the-edges operative. He could stop himself from kissing a woman.

He hoped.

She trailed her fingers down his arm and then withdrew her touch. "I wanted to kiss you on the floor of that cantina," she admitted. "Why, I don't know." Jenna shook her head. "Yes, I do. You're hot. You're dangerous. You're all the things that get my blood moving."

His pulse jumped. "So you like hot dangerous things?" he asked.

"I like you," she said, her voice quivery now. She sank down onto the chaise and looked up at him. "But liking you isn't wise. I've made a lot of bad choices in my life, and I can't do that anymore now that I have Sophie. If I fall for a guy, then it has to be the right guy, you know?"

"Sure." He wouldn't tell her that soon his job wouldn't be that dangerous. If he got that deputy director promotion, he'd be doing his shooting from behind a desk. On some level Cal would miss the fieldwork, but the deputy director job was the next step in his dream to be chief. Maybe it was best that Jenna thought his dangerous work would continue. Maybe this was the barrier they needed between them.

"Sleep," he reminded her.

Jenna lay down on the chaise and covered up. Cal was about to do the same on the floor, but his cell phone rang. He yanked it from his pocket and answered it before it could ring a second time and wake up Sophie.

"It's Kowalski," his director greeted. "What's your situation?"

Cal got up, walked across the room and stepped just outside the door and into the hall. "Is this line secure?"

"Yes. I'm using the private line in my office."

Good. That meant if there was a leak or threat from Hollywood, then at least this call wouldn't be overheard. Cal had called Kowalski right after the SUV incident, but he hadn't wanted to say too much until he knew the info would stay private.

"I'm at Ms. Laniere's estate. Were you able to get anything on that SUV that tried to run us off the road?"

"Nothing. The Texas Rangers are investigating. There was a team of them nearby searching for that missing woman, and they got there faster than the FBI."

Well, Cal wasn't holding his breath that they'd find anything related to Salazar. If the assassin had been the driver, then the first thing he would have done was ditch the vehicle. He wouldn't have wanted to drive it around with bullet holes in it.

"And what about Salazar?" Cal asked, hoping by some miracle the man had been picked up.

"He's still at large."

Cal didn't bother to groan since that was the answer he'd expected. "What about the plates?" He had made a note of them and had asked the director to run them.

"The plates weren't stolen. They were bogus."

Strange. A pro like Salazar would normally have just stolen a vehicle and then discarded it when he was done. Bogus plates took time to create. "And Hollywood? Anything new to report?"

"Nothing definitive on him, either."

Cal was afraid of that. "How did he take the news that he's under investigation?"

The director took several moments to answer. "He doesn't know."

"Excuse me?" Cal was certain he'd misunderstood the director.

"Lynch doesn't know he's being monitored. I want to let him have access to some information and see what he does with it. If he does nothing, then maybe someone has set him up."

Or maybe Hollywood knew about the monitoring and was going to play it clean for a while.

"How's Ms. Laniere?" Kowalski asked, pulling Cal's thoughts away from all the other questions.

She's making me crazy. "She's shaken up, of course." Cal used his briefing tone. Flat, unemotional, detached. Unlike the firestorm going on inside him. "My plan was to stay here with her and her child until we can make other arrangements."

"Of course." The director paused, which bothered Cal. Was Kowalski concerned about this whole paternity issue? Was he worried that Cal was going to sleep with her? Cal was worried about that, too.

"Ms. Laniere is the main reason I'm calling," Kowalski explained. "We might have another problem."

This didn't sound like a personal issue. It sounded dangerous. Besides, they didn't need another problem, personal or otherwise. They already had a boatload of them. "What's wrong now?"

"The Ranger CSI unit is at Ms. Laniere's apartment in Willow Ridge now. About a half hour ago they found a listening device near the front door. It wasn't government issue. It was something you could buy at any store that sells security equipment. Still, Lynch could have put it there."

Holden or Helena could have done the same. All three had been there. Or maybe even Gwen had done it after Jenna and he had left.

"There's more," the director continued. "I had the CSI check your car as well, and they just called to say they'd found a vehicle tracking system taped to the undercarriage."

Cal cursed. "Someone wanted to follow me." He carried that through one more step. "And that means someone could have done the same to Jenna's car."

"Probably."

"But I checked the undercarriage when I looked for explosives." Cal started for the front of the house.

"You could easily have missed it. It's small, half the size of a deck of cards. But don't let the size fool you. It might be wireless and portable, but it's still effective even at long range."

"Stay put," he called out to Jenna. "I have to go outside and check on something."

Cal hurried toward the front of the house, disengaged the security system, unlocked the front door. He drew his weapon before he hurried out into the cold night. No one seemed to be lurking in the shadows waiting to assassinate him, but he rushed. He didn't want to leave Jenna and Sophie alone for too long.

Thankfully, the overhead porch lights were enough for him to clearly see the car. Staying on the side that was nearest to the house, he stooped and looked underneath. There was no immediate sign of a tracker. But then he looked again at a clump of mud. He touched it and realized it was a fake. Plastic. He pulled it back and looked at the device beneath.

His heart dropped.

"Found it," Cal reported. "Someone camouflaged it."

"So someone wired both cars," the director concluded. "The bad news is that anyone with a laptop could have monitored your whereabouts."

Cal's heart dropped even further. Because that meant someone had tracked them to Jenna's estate.

Salazar and maybe God knows who else knew exactly where they were.

Chapter Nine

Jenna checked her watch. It was nearly 6:00 a.m. Soon, Sophie would wake up and demand her breakfast bottle.

She took a moment to gather her thoughts and to reassure herself one last time that everyone was okay. The security alarm hadn't gone off. No one had fired shots into the place. That SUV hadn't returned.

But all of those things might still happen.

Cal hadn't come out and said that, but after he'd discovered the tracking device on her car, they both knew anything was possible. He'd considered moving them again, but had decided to stay put and hope their safety measures were enough to keep out anyone who might decide to come after them.

After Cal had disarmed and removed the tracking device, every possible function of the security system had been armed. Cal had even alerted all three members of the household staff, and the gardener, Pete Spears, had assured them that he'd keep watch from the gatehouse.

All those measures had been enough. They were still alive and unharmed. But the day had barely started.

With that uncomfortable thought, Jenna eased off the chaise and moved as quietly as she could so she wouldn't wake Cal. He hadn't slept much. She knew that because he'd been awake when she finally fell asleep around midnight. He was still awake when she'd gotten up at 2:00 a.m. to feed a fussing Sophie. He'd even gone with them to the kitchen when she fixed the bottle, and he'd taken his gun with him.

But he was thankfully asleep now.

He was sitting with his legs stretched out in front of him, so his upper back and neck were resting on the chaise. His face looked perfectly relaxed, but he had his hand resting over the butt of the gun in his shoulder holster.

She reached for her shoes, but Cal's hand shot out. Before Jenna could even blink, he grabbed her wrist, turned and used the strength of his body to flatten her against the chaise.

Their eyes met.

He was on top of her with his face only

several inches away from hers. In the depths of those steel-blue eyes, she saw him process the situation. There was no emotion in those eyes. Well, not at first. Then he cursed under his breath.

"Sorry. Old habits," he mumbled.

It took her a moment to get past the shock of what'd just happened. "You mean combat training, not intimate situations?" She meant it as a joke, but it came out all wrong. Of course it did. His kisses could melt paint, and he was on top of her in what could be a good starting position for some great morning sex.

But there wouldn't be any.

Cal got off her with difficulty. He dug his knee into the chaise to lever himself up, but that created some interesting contact in their midsections.

"Dreams," he explained when he noticed that she was looking at the bulge behind the zipper of his jeans.

About me? she nearly asked but thankfully held her tongue. It was wishful thinking. Yes, he'd kissed her, but he hadn't wanted to. It'd been just a primal response. Now he wanted some distance between them. He wanted Sophie and her safe so he wouldn't feel obligated to help. And after all the trouble she'd caused for him, she couldn't blame him one bit.

Sophie's soft whimpers got her moving off the chaise but not before Cal and she exchanged uncomfortable glances. She really needed to make other security arrangements so he could leave. But that was the last thing on earth she wanted.

"Good morning, sweetheart," she greeted Sophie.

Jenna scooped her up into her arms and stole a few morning kisses. Sophie stopped fussing and gave her a wide smile. It wouldn't last, though. Soon her baby would want her bottle, so Jenna started toward the kitchen.

Cal was right behind her.

Meggie was ahead of them in the hall. The woman was walking straight toward them. "A fax just arrived for you." She handed Cal at least a dozen pages, but her attention went straight to Sophie. "I've got a bottle waiting for you, young lady."

Sophie looked at her with curious eyes and glanced up at Jenna. Jenna smiled to reassure her, and it seemed to work because Sophie smiled, too, when Meggie took her and headed for the kitchen.

Since Cal had stopped to look at the fax

and since it seemed to have grabbed his complete interest, Jenna stopped as well. "Bad news?"

"It could be." He glanced through the rest of the pages and then handed her the first one. "These are reports I requested from my director. I asked for a background on Gwen Mitchell and I also wanted him to look for any suspicious activity that could be linked back to you."

She skimmed through the page and groaned. "There was a break-in at the pediatrician's office. Sophie's file was stolen." Jenna smacked the paper against the palm of her hand. "Holden is responsible for this. He's trying to prove that Paul's the father."

"What would have been in that file?" Cal asked.

"Well, certainly no DNA information, but her blood type was listed. It's O-positive."

Cal actually looked conflicted. "O-positive is the most common. It's my blood type."

Jenna immediately understood his mixed emotions. This might make Holden think she was telling the truth about Cal being Sophie's father. But this would also make his director have more doubts. She really did need to get a DNA test done right away.

Cal made his way toward the kitchen while he continued to read the fax. "Gwen Mitchell's been a freelance investigative reporter for ten years." He shuffled through the pages. "She's gotten some pretty tough stories, including one on a mob boss. And a Colombian drug dealer."

So they weren't dealing with an amateur. "She doesn't sound like the type of person to back off."

"She's not," Cal confirmed. He stopped again just outside the kitchen entrance. "According to this, when Gwen was working on that story in Colombia, a woman was killed."

Jenna nearly gasped. "Gwen murdered her?"

"Not exactly, but she was responsible for the woman's death. Gwen made the drug lord believe this woman had revealed sensitive information. The drug lord had her killed. Gwen managed to record the actual murder and that became the centerpiece of her story."

"Oh, God." So this was what they were up against. A ruthless woman who'd do whatever was necessary to get her story. And in this case her story was getting Jenna. Gwen would do anything to collect the one million dollars that Paul had offered her.

Cal walked ahead of her and checked the

security system. It was identical to the check he'd made before and after Sophie's 2:00 a.m. feeding. When he was satisfied that everything was still secure, they went to the kitchen.

Meggie had Sophie in the crook of her arm and was trying to feed her a bottle while she checked something on the stove. Jenna went to take the child, but Cal caught her.

"I'll take her. You need to eat something."

Jenna's stomach chose that exact moment to growl. She couldn't argue with that. But she was more than a little surprised when Cal so easily took Sophie from Meggie. He sat down at the kitchen table and readjusted the bottle so there'd be an even flow of formula.

Jenna and Meggie exchanged glances.

"You're sure you haven't done baby duty before?" Jenna asked. She poured herself a cup of coffee, and Meggie dished her up some scrambled eggs.

"Nope," he assured her.

He was a natural. He seemed so at ease with Sophie. And willing to help. It made Jenna feel guilty—his willingness could be costly for him. If she hadn't told that lie to Holden, Cal would never have come to Willow Ridge, and he wouldn't be in this dangerous situation now. Of course, Jenna was thankful he was there. For Sophie's sake. But she hated what she'd done to him.

Jenna had only managed to eat one bite of the eggs when a shrill beep pulsed through the room. It brought Cal to his feet. He handed Sophie to her and drew his gun.

Just like that, her heart went into overdrive, and her stomach knotted. Jenna passed her daughter to Meggie so she could go with Cal and see what had happened to trigger the surveillance system.

Cal hurried to the security panel just as his cell phone rang. He answered it while he opened the panel box.

"You're here at the estate?" he asked a moment later. That sent him to the side windows by the front door, and he looked out. "Something's wrong."

It wasn't a question, but he must have gotten an answer because he hung up.

"Director Kowalski just arrived," Cal relayed to her. "He found Holden and Helena Carr outside. They were trying to get in the front gate."

CAL HAD HOPED that today wouldn't be as insane as the day before, but it wasn't off to a good start. Here it was, barely dawn, his director had arrived for an impromptu visit, and two of their suspects were only yards away. Cal didn't want those two in the same state with Jenna and Sophie, yet here they were.

Had they been the ones to put the tracking devices on Jenna's and his vehicles? Maybe. Or maybe they'd merely benefited from what someone else had done.

"Can your director arrest Holden and Helena?" Jenna asked.

"Probably not. I'm sure they'll have a cover story for their attempt to get through the front gate."

But maybe they could call the local authorities and have them picked up for trespassing. It wouldn't keep the duo in jail long since they'd have no trouble making bail, but it would send a message that they couldn't continue to intimidate Jenna without paying a consequence or two.

Cal grabbed his jacket and disarmed the security system so he could go outside and *greet* their visitors. Jenna picked up her jacket as well.

"I want to talk to them," she said before he could object to her going with him.

"That wouldn't be wise."

"On the contrary. I want them to know I

won't cower in fear or hide. I want them out of my life."

Cal wasn't sure this was the way to make that happen, but he didn't want to take the time to argue with her. Director Kowalski might need backup.

"Wait on the porch," he instructed. "That way, they can see you, but you can get back inside if things turn ugly."

He hoped like the devil that she obeyed.

Cal walked down the steps and spotted the gardener, Pete, in the gatehouse. He was armed with a shotgun. Good. He'd take all the help he could get.

There were three cars just on the other side of the gate. Two were high-end luxury vehicles, no doubt belonging to Holden and Helena. Cal wondered why they hadn't driven together. The third vehicle was a standard-issue four-wheel-drive from ISA's motor pool.

The three drivers were at the gate, waiting. Cal didn't like the idea of his director being locked out with the Carrs, but he couldn't risk Sophie's and Jenna's safety. He needed to keep that gate closed until he was sure this visit wasn't going to lead to an attack.

Before he approached the gate, Cal glanced

over his shoulder. Amazingly, Jenna was still on the porch. He doubted she'd stay there, but he welcomed these few minutes of safety.

"I didn't try to break in," Helena volunteered. "I merely wanted to speak to Jenna, and I was trying to find an intercom or something when that man with the shotgun sounded the alarm."

Kowalski was behind her. He had his weapon drawn in his right hand and held an equipment bag in his left. He rolled his eyes, an indication he didn't buy Helena's story.

Holden's eyes, however, were much more intense. He had his attention fastened to Jenna on the porch. "I need to talk to her, too," he insisted.

I, not *we.* Given the fact that the siblings had arrived in separate vehicles, perhaps they were in the middle of a family squabble. Considering what Helena had said at Jenna's apartment in Willow Ridge, that didn't surprise Cal.

"Jenna's not receiving visitors," Cal said sarcastically. "But I'll pass along any message."

Holden continued to watch Jenna. "The message is that she's in grave danger." His voice was probably loud enough for her to hear.

Cal shrugged. "Old news."

"Not exactly," Holden challenged. He glanced at his sister.

Now it was Helena's turn to show some intensity. Anger tightened the muscles on her face. "My brother broke into my personal computer and read the e-mail Paul's attorney sent me. Holden seems to think that I'd be willing to do whatever Paul wants me to do."

Well, this had potential. "And what does Paul want you to do?"

Helena came closer and hooked her perfectly manicured fingers around the wrought-iron spindles that made up the gate front. "Paul seemed to believe that I would tie up loose ends if Salazar failed."

Holden stepped forward as well. "My sister's orders are to kill us all once Salazar has Sophie."

Oh, hell. Paul really had put together some plan. Kidnapping and murder.

"I'm not a killer," Helena said, her voice shaky now. "I have no idea why Paul thought I would do this."

"Don't you?" Holden again. He aimed his answer at Cal. "My sister was sleeping with Paul. She didn't think I knew, but I did. And I also knew that they had plans to kill Jenna if she turned down his marriage proposal."

"That's not true," Helena protested.

Cal heard footsteps behind him and

groaned. A glance over his shoulder confirmed that Jenna wanted to be part of this conversation. He didn't blame her. But he also wanted to keep her safe. He positioned himself in front of her, hoping that would be enough if bullets started flying.

"Paul didn't love me," Helena said to Jenna. She shook her head. "He didn't love you, either."

"I know," Jenna readily agreed. "He wanted my business. And you were in on his plan to get it?"

"Only the business." Helena's face flushed as if she was embarrassed by the admission of her guilt. "I never would have agreed to murder."

Cal wasn't sure he believed her. A flushed face could be faked. "How does Gwen Mitchell fit into the picture?" he asked.

Helena's eyes widened. "The reporter?"

"Yeah. Paul was sleeping with her, too." It was a good guess. After reading Gwen's background, Cal figured she'd do anything to get a story.

Helena shook her head again and a thin stream of breath left her mouth. "I didn't know."

"So Paul slept around," Holden snarled. If he

had any concern for his sister's reaction, he didn't show it. "I don't think that's nearly as important as the fact that he's put bounties on our heads." Holden cursed. "He was my friend. Like a brother to me. And this is what he does?"

Kowalski came closer. "What exactly did Paul say in the e-mail he sent you?" he asked Holden.

Holden sent a nasty glare the director's way. "Well, he didn't ask me to kill anyone, that's for sure. He asked me to check on some accounts and old business connections. Nothing illegal. Nothing sinister. Obviously, Helena can't say the same. Paul made some kind of arrangement with my sister—"

"He didn't," Helena practically shouted. "And I didn't agree to do what he asked." She caught her brother's arm and whirled him around so he was facing her. "Have you ever considered that he could be doing this for some other reason? To get us at each other's throats? Paul had a sick sense of humor, and this might be his idea of a joke."

"My daughter is in danger," Jenna said, drawing everyone's attention back to her. "It's not a joke. Salazar is out there, and Paul is the one who sent him after Sophie."

Cal glanced at Holden and Helena to see

their reactions. They were still hurling daggers at each other. It was a good time to interject some logic in this game of pointing fingers.

"If Paul wanted Sophie, but he also wanted all of you dead, then who would be left to raise her?" the director challenged. "Who would be left to manage his estate? Why would he want to eliminate the very people who could give him some postmortem help?"

Dead silence.

"Maybe he expected Gwen Mitchell to help him," Jenna mumbled. "Maybe they were more than just lovers."

That was exactly what Cal was considering. Gwen's ruthlessness would have endeared her to Paul. And for that matter, the e-mails could be a hoax. A way to drive them all apart. Gwen could have further instructions that Paul could have given her before he was murdered.

And that brought Cal back to something he wanted to ask. "How exactly did you two know that Jenna would be here?"

Holden shrugged and peeled off the leather glove on his left hand. "It wasn't a lucky guess, was it, Helena?"

The woman's shoulders snapped back, but she didn't answer her brother. She looked at Cal instead. "Salazar called me a few hours ago to tell me that he'd put a tracking device on Jenna's car. He said she was here."

Cal silently cursed and glanced around to make sure Salazar wasn't lurking somewhere. "Go back in the house," he instructed Jenna in a whisper. "Arm the security system."

"But if it isn't safe for me, it isn't safe for you," Jenna pointed out, also in a whisper.

"I won't be long," he promised, knowing that didn't really address her concerns. Still, he had some unfinished business. Concerns about his personal safety could wait.

"What else did Salazar say?" Kowalski demanded from Helena once Jenna started for the house.

"Nothing. I swear. He told me about the tracking device, said Jenna was at the estate, and that was it. He hung up." She slid an icy glance at her brother. "I didn't know Holden had tapped my calls. Not until I arrived here and realized that he'd followed me."

Cal stared at Holden, to see if he would add anything, or at least offer an explanation as to why he'd eavesdropped on his sister's conversations. But maybe this was the way it'd always been between them.

"You're not getting into the estate," Cal assured both of them. "You're trespassing."

Holden smacked the glove against the gate. "Arrest me, then. Go ahead. Waste your time when what you should be doing is stopping Salazar."

"Oh, I intend to do that." And he intended to stop Gwen if she was as neck deep in this as he thought she was.

"I don't think it'll be a waste of time if you report to the local FBI office for questioning," the director interjected.

"When there's a warrant for my arrest, I'll show up," Holden snarled. He headed for his car, got in and drove away. His tires squealed from the excessive speed.

"I'll go in for questioning," Helena told Kowalski. Her eyes watered with tears. "I'll do whatever's necessary to keep us all alive."

"Paul asked you to kill us," Cal reminded her. "What makes you think you're in danger?"

She glanced at her brother's car as it quickly disappeared down the road. "Holden won't show me the e-mail he got from Paul. My brother doesn't trust me. And why should he? Because of Paul, Holden thinks I'll try to kill him, and he's no doubt trying to figure out how to kill me first before I can carry through with Paul's wishes."

With that, she walked to her car. Her shoulders were slumped, and she swiped her hand over her cheek to wipe away her tears.

"Any idea what was in Holden's e-mail?" Cal asked once Helena had driven away.

Kowalski shook his head. "We're still working on that. But Helena didn't lie when she said what was in hers. Paul did leave orders to kill Jenna, Holden and anyone else who got in the way of Salazar taking the baby."

Anyone else. That would be Cal. Somehow he would stop Salazar and unravel this mess that'd brought danger right to Jenna's doorstep.

He reached over and hit the control switch to open the gate. Kowalski walked closer and handed him an equipment bag. "I figured you might need this. There's an extra weapon, ammo and a clean laptop."

Cal appreciated the supplies, but knowing Salazar could be out there, he continued to keep watch. So did Pete. The lanky man with sandy blond hair shifted his shotgun and wary gaze all around the grounds. There weren't many places Salazar could take cover and use an assault rifle. Unless he actually made it onto the property. Then there were a lot of places he could use to launch an attack.

Cal glanced down into the unzipped bag

and then looked at Kowalski. "Does this mean I'll be here for a while?"

"For now." He paused. "I know it's not protocol. Hell, it's not even legal. That's why you can't be here in a professional capacity. This is personal, understand? You're on an official leave of absence."

"I understand."

It was the truth. This had become personal for Cal.

"Last night after we talked, I worked to set up a safe house for Ms. Laniere and her child," Kowalski explained. "But then the communications monitor at headquarters informed me that my account might have been compromised. There was something suspicious about the way info was feeding in and out of what was supposed to be a secure computer. That means someone might have seen the message traffic on the safe house."

Cal cursed. "Hollywood?"

"Maybe. But it could also be a false alarm caused by a computer glitch. That's why I decided to come in person and tell you to stay put for now."

That's what Cal was afraid he was going to say. "But Salazar knows where Jenna is."

Kowalski nodded. "You might have to take

him out if we can't stop him first. The FBI and the Rangers are looking for him. They know he's probably in the area."

Yeah. And for that reason, Cal didn't want to leave Jenna alone for too long. "I'll do what's necessary."

Another nod. The director glanced around uneasily. "What about the paternity issue? Did you get that DNA test done to prove you aren't the baby's father?"

Cal hadn't forgotten about that, but it was definitely on the back burner. "I figured it could wait until all of this is over. Besides, I want Holden and Salazar to believe the child is mine. That might get them to back off."

Though that was more than a long shot. Things had already been set into motion, and it would take a miracle to stop them.

Kowalski met him eye-to-eye. "You're sure that's the only reason you're putting off a DNA test?"

Cal stared at him and tried not to blast the man for accusing him of lying. "I've never given you a reason to distrust me."

"You have now." The director turned and started for his vehicle. "Clear up this paternity issue, Cal, before it destroys everything you've worked so hard to get."

There was just one problem with clearing it up. Well, two.

Jenna and Sophie.

He closed the gate and stood there watching his boss drive away. Cal wondered if his chances at that promotion had just driven away, too. Without Kowalski's blessing, Cal wasn't going to get that deputy director job. Not a chance. He wouldn't even have a career left to salvage.

Cal grabbed the equipment bag and went back to the house. Jenna was there, waiting for him just inside the door. A few feet behind her was Meggie. She had Sophie cradled in her arms. The little girl smiled at him. She was too young and innocent to know the danger she was in.

Seeing Jenna and the baby was a reminder that his career was pretty damn small in the grand scheme of things.

"So, are we going on the run again?" Jenna began to nibble on her bottom lip.

"No." He hoped that was the right thing to do.

Still, he wasn't going to put full trust in his director's decision for them to stay put because Hollywood might still be getting access to any- and everything.

"I need backup," Cal mumbled to himself. More than just a gardener with a shotgun.

And it had to be someone he trusted.

His brother Max was his first choice. If Max was on assignment, then he'd call a friend who owned a personal protection agency. One way or another he wanted someone reliable on the grounds ASAP, and these were men he could trust with his life.

"So we stay put," Jenna concluded. She paused. "And then what?"

"We prepare ourselves for the worst."

Because the worst was on the way.

Chapter Ten

"Rule one," Cal said to Jenna. He slipped on her eye goggles and adjusted them so they fit firmly on her face. "Treat all firearms as if they're loaded."

He positioned the Smith & Wesson 9 mm gun in her hand and turned her toward the target. It was the silhouette of a person rather than a bull's-eye. Jenna didn't like the idea of aiming at a person, real or otherwise, but she also knew this was necessary. Cal was doing everything humanly possible to keep her and Sophie safe. She wanted to do her part as well.

"Rule two," he continued. "Never point a weapon at anything or anyone you don't intend to destroy."

There it was in a nutshell. Her biggest fear. She'd have to kill someone to stop all of this insanity.

Every precaution was being taken to

prevent anyone, especially Salazar, from gaining access to the estate. Cal's friend Jordan Taylor had arrived an hour earlier. He was an expert in security. Jenna hadn't actually met or seen the man because he'd immediately gotten to work on installing monitoring equipment around the entire fence. Jordan had brought another man, Cody Guillory, with him, and the two were going to patrol the grounds. In the meantime, Director Kowalski and the FBI had assured Cal they were doing everything to catch Salazar and neutralize the threat.

However, Cal had insisted she learn how to shoot, just in case.

Jenna hadn't balked at his suggestion, but she had waited until Sophie was down for her morning nap. Meggie and the baby were in the nursery with the door locked, Meggie was armed and the rest of the house was on lockdown. No one was to get in or out.

"Rule three—don't hold your gun sideways. Only stupid people trying to look cool do that. It'll give you a bad aim and cause you to miss your target." Cal moved behind her.

Touching her.

Something he'd been doing since this

lesson started. Of course, it was impossible to give a shooting lesson without touching, but the contact made it hard for her to concentrate. It reminded her of their kiss and the fact that she wanted him to touch her. She needed therapy. How could she be thinking about such things at a time like this?

Quite easily, she admitted.

It was Cal and his superhero outfit. Camo pants, black chest-hugging T-shirt. Steel-toed boots. The clothes had been in the equipment bag that the director had delivered, and in this case, the clothes made the man. Well, they made her notice every inch of his body, anyway.

"Okay, here we go," he said, pulling her attention back to the lesson. "Feet apart." He put his hand on the inside of her thigh, just above her knee, to position her.

A shiver of heat went through her.

"Left foot slightly in front. Right elbow completely straight. Since you're new at this, look at the target with your right eye. Close your left one. It'll make it easier to aim." He stopped with his hand beneath her straight elbow and his arm grazing her breasts. "You're shaking a little. Are you cold?"

The room was a little chilly, but that

wasn't it. Jenna knew she should just lie. It was right there on the tip of her tongue, but she made the mistake of glancing at him. Even through the goggles, he had no trouble seeing her expression.

"Oh," he mumbled. "Some women get turned on from shooting. All that power in their hands."

Jenna continued to stare at him. "I don't think it's the gun." She probably should have lied about that, too.

Cal chuckled. It was husky, deep and totally male. He dropped his hands to her waist to readjust her stance. At least that's how it started, but he kept his hands there and pressed against her. His front against her back.

That didn't help the shaking. Nor did it cool down the heat.

He grabbed two sets of earmuffs, put one on her and slipped the other on himself. "Take aim at the center of the target," he said, his voice loud so that she could hear him. "Squeeze the trigger with gentle but steady pressure."

Which was exactly what he was doing to her waist.

"Now?" she asked.

"Whenever you're ready." He brushed against her butt.

Sheez. Since this lesson was turning into foreplay, Jenna decided to go ahead. She thought through all of Cal's instructions and then pulled the trigger. Even with the earmuffs, the shot was loud, and her entire right arm recoiled.

She pulled off the earmuffs and goggles and had a look at where her shot had landed.

"That'll work," Cal assured her.

Jenna looked closer at the target and frowned. "I hit the guy in his family jewels."

Cal chuckled again. "Trust me, that'll work."

She replaced the earmuffs and goggles so she could try more shots. She adjusted her aim but the bullet went low again. It took her three more tries before she got a shot anywhere near the upper torso.

"I think you got the hang of it," Cal praised. He took off his own muffs and laid them back on the shelf. He did the same to hers and then took the gun from her. It wasn't easy—her fingers had frozen around it.

"You did good," he added, making eye contact with her.

His hand went around the back of her neck, pulling her to him, and his mouth went to hers.

Yes! she thought. *Finally!*

Maybe it was the fact she was a new mother and had learned to appreciate what little free time she had, but Jenna wanted to make the most of these stolen moments.

Cal obviously did, too. He kissed her, hungry and hot, as if he'd been waiting all morning to do just that.

He ran his hand into her hair so that he controlled the movement of her head. She didn't mind. He angled her so that he could deepen the kiss. And just like that, she was starved for more of him.

With his hands and mouth on her, Jenna's back landed against one of the smooth, square floor-to-ceiling columns that set off the firing lane. Cal landed against her. All those firm sinewy muscles in his chest played havoc with her breasts. It'd been so long since she'd been in a man's arms, and this man had been worth the wait.

His mouth teased and coaxed her. The not so gentle pressure of his chest muscles and pecs made her latch on to him and pull him even closer, until they were fitted together exactly the way a man and woman should fit. They still had their clothes on, but Jenna had no trouble imagining what it would be like to have Cal naked and inside her.

Her need for him was almost embarrassing. She'd never been a sexually charged person. She preferred a good kiss to sex, probably because she'd never actually had good sex. But something told her that she wouldn't have to settle for one or the other with Cal. He was more than capable of delivering both.

He slid his hand down her side, to the bottom of her stretchy top, and lifted it. His fingers, which were just as hot and clever as his mouth, were suddenly on her bare skin, making their way to her breasts and jerking down the cups of her bra.

Everything intensified. His touch. The heat. That primal tug deep within her.

Cal pulled back from the kiss, only so he could wet his fingertips with his tongue. For a moment, she didn't understand why. But then his mouth came back to hers, and those slick wet fingers went to her nipples. He caressed her, and gently pinched her nipples, bringing them to peaks.

Jenna nearly lost it right there.

Frantically searching for some relief to the pressure-cooker heat, she hooked her fingers through the belt loops of his camo pants and dragged him to her, so that his hard sex ground against the soft, wet part of her body.

It was good. Too good.

Because it only made her want the rest of him.

She reached for his zipper, but Cal clamped his hand over hers. Stopping her. "No condom," he reminded her.

Jenna cursed, both thankful and angry that he'd managed to keep a clear head. She didn't want a clear head. She wanted Cal. But she also knew he was right. They couldn't risk having unprotected sex.

She tried to calm down. She'd been ready to climax, and her body wasn't pleased that it wasn't going to get what it wanted.

Cal, however, didn't let her come down. He pinned her in place against the column and shoved down her zipper. He didn't wait to see how she would react to that. He kissed her again. And again, the heat began to soar.

While he did some clever things with his mouth, he tormented her nipples with his left hand. But it was his right hand that sent her soaring. It slid into her jeans. Underneath her panties. He wasn't gentle, wasn't slow. His middle and index fingers eased into the slippery heat of her body and moved.

It didn't take much. Just a few of those clever strokes. Another deep French kiss. He nipped her nipple with his fingertips.

Their kiss muffled the sound she made, and his fingers continued to move, to give her every last bit of pleasure he could.

CAL CAUGHT HER to make sure she didn't fall. Jenna buried her face against the crook of his neck and let him catch her. Her breath came out in rough, hot jolts. Her body was trembling, her face, flushed with arousal.

She smelled like sex.

It was a powerful scent that urged his body to do a lot more than he'd just done. Of course, what he'd done was too much. He'd crossed lines that shouldn't have been crossed. In fact, he'd gone just short of what his director already suspected him of doing.

A husky laugh rumbled in Jenna's throat, and she blinked as if to clear her vision. Cal certainly needed to clear his. He made sure she was steady on her feet, and then he zipped up her jeans so he could step away from her.

She blinked again. This time, she looked confused, then embarrassed. "Oh, mercy. You could get into trouble for that."

He shrugged and left it at that.

"I keep forgetting that this has much stiffer consequences for you than it does for me." Still breathing hard, she pushed the wisps of blond hair from her face. A natural blonde. He'd discovered that when he unzipped her pants and pushed down her panties.

Now he needed to forget what he'd seen.

Hell. He just needed to forget, period.

"Of course, I'll get a broken heart out of this," she mumbled, and fixed her jeans.

A broken heart?

Did that mean she had feelings for him?

"Forget I said that," she mumbled a moment later. She looked even more embarrassed. "I'm not making sense right now."

So no broken heart. But still Cal had to wonder....

He didn't have long to wonder because his phone rang. The caller ID screen indicated it was Jordan.

"I was beefing up security by the front gate when a car pulled up," Jordan explained in the no-nonsense tone that Cal had always heard him use. "You have a visitor. She says her name is Gwen Mitchell and that she *must* talk to you."

"Gwen Mitchell's out front," Cal relayed to Jenna.

He wasn't exactly surprised. Everyone seemed to know where they were. But how should he handle this visit? He needed to question Gwen, but he didn't want to do that by placing Jenna and Sophie at risk.

"She says she has some new information you should hear," Jordan added. "She's refused to give it to me, but I can get it if you like. What do you want me to do with her?"

From Jordan, it was a formidable question. If Gwen had any inkling of the dangerous man that Jordan could be, she probably would have been running for the hills. Jordan was loyal to the end. He and Cal were close enough that he would trust Jordan to kill for him. Of course, he hoped killing Gwen wouldn't be necessary.

"Make sure she's not armed," Cal instructed. "And then escort her to the porch. I'll meet you at the front door."

"You're not going to let her in the house?" Jordan challenged.

"Not a chance."

Cal believed Gwen wanted one thing. A story. And even though he could relate to her devotion to duty, he was beginning to see that as a huge risk.

"You're meeting with her?" Jenna asked, following right behind him.

Cal locked the gun room door, using the key that Jenna had given him earlier. "I have a hunch that Gwen knows a lot more than she's saying. Plus, I want to hear what she considers to be important information."

"It could be a trap," Jenna pointed out.

"It could be, but if so, it's suicide. Jordan won't let an armed suspect make it to the door. Still, I want you to wait inside."

She huffed. For such a simple sound, it conveyed a lot. Jenna didn't like losing control of her life. But one way or another he was going to protect her.

"I'll stay in the foyer," she bargained. "Because you aren't actually going outside, are you?" She didn't wait for him to confirm that. "Besides, any information she has would pertain to me. Paul sent her after me because he thought I planned to murder him. I deserve to hear what she has to say."

He stopped at the front door, whirled around and stared at her. He had already geared up for an argument about why she shouldn't be present at this meeting, but Jenna pressed her fingers over his mouth.

"Don't let sexual attraction for me get in the way of doing what's smart," she said. Except it sounded like some kind of accusation.

"The sexual attraction isn't making me stupid."

"If you didn't want me in your bed," Jenna continued, "then you wouldn't be so protective of me. You'd let me confront Gwen." She frowned when he scowled at her. "Or you'd at least let me listen to what she has to say. I can do that as safely as you can. You already pointed out that Jordan will make sure Gwen isn't armed."

True. So why did he still feel the need to shelter Jenna from this conversation?

Hell. The attraction he felt for her could really complicate everything.

Cal scowled and threw open the front door.

Gwen was there, looking not at all certain of what she might have gotten herself into. Jordan probably had something to do with that. At six-two and a hundred and ninety pounds, he was no lightweight. He stood behind Gwen, looming over her. He was armed and had an extra weapon on his utility belt. In addition, he had a small communicator fitted into his left ear. He was no doubt getting updates from an associate somewhere on the grounds.

Jordan seemed to be doing a good job of neutralizing any threat from Gwen, but Cal took it one step further and made sure he was in front of Jenna.

"There's someone else waiting by the gate," Jordan informed them. "Archie Monroe. His ID looks legit. Says he's from Cryogen Labs."

Cal went on instant alert, and motioned for Jordan to come inside. He shut the door, leaving Gwen standing outside, and lowered his voice to a whisper. "Could it be Salazar?"

"Not unless he's had major cosmetic surgery. This guy's about sixty, gray hair and he's got a couple of spare tires around his middle."

"It's not Salazar," Jenna provided. Jordan and Cal stared at her. "He's a lab technician. I called Cryogen this morning and asked them to send out someone to do a DNA test on Sophie."

Cal choked back a groan and geared himself up for an argument.

Jenna beat him to it. "The DNA issue is hurting your career. I can't let it continue."

Cal opened his mouth. Then he closed it and tried to get hold of his temper. "I will not let you put my job ahead of Sophie's safety. Got that?" Then he turned to Jordan. "Tell him there's been a misunderstanding, that his services are not needed."

Jordan nodded and opened the door to hurry toward the front gate. Jenna didn't say anything else, but she did send Cal a disapproving look. He knew she didn't want this test. Not really. She wouldn't want to do anything to increase the risk of danger for Sophie. That's what made it even more frustrating.

She was doing this for him.

That attraction had *really* screwed up things between them.

"Is there a problem?" Gwen asked, glancing over her shoulder at Jordan, who was making his way to the lab tech.

"You tell me," Cal challenged. "Why are you here?"

Gwen's attention went to Jenna. "I know you didn't murder Paul."

Not exactly a revelation.

"That's why you came?" Jenna stepped closer. "To tell me something I already know?"

"I have proof. I got Paul's attorney to e-mail me surveillance videos. There's not any actual footage of Paul being killed, but there is footage of you leaving the estate. Fifteen minutes later, there's footage of Paul coming out of his office to get something and then returning."

Cal knew all about that surveillance. The ISA had studied and restudied it. Well, Hollywood had. And Cal had reviewed it to make sure Jenna hadn't been the killer. The surveillance hadn't captured images of the person who'd entered Paul's office and shot him in the back of the head. Thermal images taken with ISA equipment had shown a person entering through a private entrance. No security camera had been set up there. Of course, the killer had to have known that.

"You could have called Jenna to tell her this," Cal pointed out.

Gwen shook her head. Her eyes showed stress. They were bloodshot and had smudgy dark circles beneath. "I think someone's listening in on my conversations. Someone's following me, too. I think it's because I'm getting close to unraveling all of this."

"Or maybe you're faking all this to cover your own guilt," Jenna countered.

Gwen didn't look offended. She merely nodded. "I could be, but I'm not." She gave a weary sigh. "I think there's a problem with the e-mails Paul wanted us all to receive."

"I'm listening," Cal said when she paused.

"I've been talking to Paul's attorney, and he told me that Paul wrote many e-mails and left instructions as to which to send out. For instance, if Jenna had had a baby, he was to send out set three. If any one of us, Jenna, Holden, Helena or Salazar, was dead by the time of the send-out date, then a different set was to be e-mailed."

"So?" Cal challenged. This wasn't news, either.

"So it wasn't the lawyer who determined which set was to go out. It was Holden."

"Holden?" he and Jenna said in unison. Whoa. Now, *that* was news.

"I asked him, and he confirmed it. But he said he had no idea what was in the other e-mails. He claims that they were encrypted when they went out and that in Paul's instructions to him, he asked Holden not to try to decode them, that he wanted each e-mail to be personal and private."

Well, that added a new twist, not that Cal needed this information to suspect Holden. Holden had a lot to gain from this situation, especially if he wanted to make sure he didn't have to share Paul's estate with his sister or any potential heirs.

But then, Gwen had motive, too. It could be that she just wanted a good story from all of this, but Paul had offered her a million dollars to find his killer. That was a lot of incentive to put a plan together. And there was another possibility: that Gwen hadn't just been involved in Paul's life but also his death.

Cal decided to go with an old-fashioned bluff.

"You didn't have any trouble getting Paul's lawyer to cooperate." He made a knowing sound. "Did you meet him when you were pretending to be Paul's maid? Are you the infamous Mary? And before you think about lying to me, you should probably know that I just read a very interesting intel report from an insider in Monte de Leon." That was a lie, of course, but Cal thought it would pay off.

Gwen's eyes widened, and she went a little pale. "Yes, I was Mary. I faked a résumé to get a job at Paul's estate, but he quickly figured out who I was."

The bluff had worked. Cal continued to push. "Is that when you killed him?"

"No." More color drained from her face, and she repeated that denial. "I didn't kill Paul."

"And why should I believe you?" Cal pressed.

"Because killing him wouldn't have helped me get a story. I wanted the insider's view to Paul's business. With him dead, my story was dead, too."

"Now you've resurrected it with a new

angle. You don't care that you're putting Jenna and her daughter in danger?"

"I don't know what you mean." Gwen's voice wavered. "I haven't put them in danger."

"Haven't you?" Jenna asked, stepping closer so that she was practically in Gwen's face.

"Not intentionally." She seemed sincere. Of course, she was a reporter after a story, so Cal wasn't buying it.

Cal saw something over Gwen's shoulder, and he re-aimed his gun. But it was Jordan, who was quickly making his way back to the porch.

"Hell. It's like Grand Central Terminal around here," Jordan grumbled. "I sent the lab guy on his way, but someone else just drove up. He says his name is Mark Lynch. Hollywood. And he wants to see all three of you."

Gwen flattened her hand on her chest. "Me?"

"Especially you."

Chapter Eleven

Jenna didn't know which surprised her more—that Hollywood had shown up or that he wanted to see Gwen. It was definitely a development that she hadn't seen coming. It could be very dangerous.

Her first instinct was to tell Jordan to stop Hollywood from getting any closer to the house. Sophie would be waking from her nap at any minute, and even though Meggie had instructions not to leave the nursery until she checked with them, if they let Hollywood in the gate, he would be too close to her baby.

Gwen was already too close.

"We could take this meeting to the gatehouse," Jenna suggested. That way, they could ask Hollywood how he knew Gwen and why he wanted to see her. Or why he wanted to see

Cal and her, for that matter. Even though he didn't know it, he was a suspect.

Cal glanced at her. She knew that look. He was trying to figure out how to make this meeting happen so that she wasn't part of it.

"Hollywood asked to see me, too," Jenna reminded him.

"People don't always get what they want," Cal responded.

Before Jenna could challenge that, Gwen interrupted. "I don't want to see him." She managed to look indignant. Angry, even. "He's going to tell you that I'm behind the attempt to kill you. It's not true."

"Why would he tell us that?" Jenna demanded.

Silence. Gwen glanced over her shoulder as if to verify that Hollywood's car was indeed there.

"We'll go to the gatehouse," Cal insisted. "I'm interested in what Hollywood has to say about you. And himself." He turned to Jenna and took his backup weapon from an ankle holster. Cal handed it to her. "Stay close to me."

She nodded, taking the weapon as confidently as she could. Jenna didn't want Gwen to know that she didn't have much experience handling a gun.

Jenna also silently thanked Cal for not giving her a hassle about attending this impromptu meeting. That couldn't have been easy for him. His training made him want to keep her tucked away so she'd be safer. Part of Jenna wanted that, too. But more than her own safety, she wanted to get to the truth that would ultimately get her daughter out of danger.

Cal locked the front door before they stepped away from it. The chilly wind whipped at them as they went down the porch steps and across the front yard. Both Cal and Jordan shot glances around the estate, both of them looking for any kind of threat. However, Jenna felt their biggest threat was the man waiting on the other side of the gate.

Hollywood was there with his hands clamped around the wrought-iron rods. He stepped back when Jordan entered the code to open the gate.

"Thanks for seeing me," Hollywood greeted Cal. He volleyed glances at all of them, except for Gwen. He tossed her a venomous glare.

Jordan stepped forward, motioning for Hollywood to lift his arms, and searched him. He extracted a gun from a shoulder holster hidden beneath Hollywood's leather jacket. Hollywood didn't protest being disarmed. He merely followed Cal's direction when Cal motioned for him to go inside the gatehouse.

The building was small. It obviously wasn't meant for meetings, but Cal, Gwen and Jenna followed Hollywood inside. Jordan waited just outside the door with his body angled so that he could see both them and the house. Good. Jenna didn't want anyone trying to sneak in.

Hollywood aimed his index finger at Gwen. "Anything she says about me is a lie."

"Funny, she said the same thing about you," Cal commented.

"Of course she did. She wants to cover her butt."

"And you don't?" Gwen challenged.

Jenna decided this was a good time to stand back and listen. These two intended to clear the air, and that could give them information about what the heck was going on.

"I slept with her last year in Monte de Leon," Hollywood confessed to Cal. "And when I told her it couldn't be anything more than a one-night stand, she didn't take it well. I figured she'd be out to get me. She's the one who's setting me up. She wants to make it look as if I've been feeding information to Salazar."

"Don't flatter yourself." Gwen took a step closer and got right in Hollywood's face. "I wasn't upset about the breakup. I was upset with myself that I let it happen in the first place."

Hollywood cursed. "You planned it all. You came on to me with the hopes I'd give you information about the ISA's investigation into Paul's illegal activities."

"I slept with you because I'd had too much to drink," Gwen tossed back.

Hollywood didn't have a comeback for that. He stood there, seething, his hands balled into fists and veins popping out on his forehead.

"So you slept with both Paul and Hollywood around the same time?" Jenna asked the woman.

Gwen nodded and had the decency to blush, especially since her affair with Paul had been a calculating way to get her story. That meant Hollywood might be telling the truth about Gwen's motives. But he still could have leaked information.

"How exactly could Gwen have set you up?" Cal asked, taking the words out of Jenna's mouth.

"I think she stole my access code and

password while she was in my hotel room in Monte de Leon."

Jenna looked at Gwen, who didn't deny or confirm anything. But she did dodge Jenna's gaze.

"You reported that the code and password could have been compromised?" Cal asked.

"No. I didn't know they had been. Not until yesterday when I figured out that someone was tapping into classified information. I knew it wouldn't take long for Kowalski to think I was the one doing it."

"And you aren't?" Jenna asked point-blank.

"I'm not." There was no hesitation. No hint of guilt. Just frustration. But maybe Hollywood was true to his nickname—this could be just good acting.

"There's a lot going on," Hollywood continued. "Someone is pulling a lot of strings to manipulate this situation. Gwen wants a story, and she wants it to be big. That's why she's stirring the pot. That's why these crazy things are happening to all of us."

"Someone is out to get us," Cal clarified. "Someone tried to run me and Jenna off the road last night. And someone planted a tracking device on her car. You think Gwen is responsible for that?"

"Well, it wasn't me. I stayed back in Willow Ridge to look for that missing woman, Kinley Ford. Heck, I even called the FBI from town to let them know I'd learned the woman had been there. You can check cell tower records to confirm that."

Not really. Because with Hollywood's expertise, he could have figured out a way around that.

Hollywood swore under his breath and shook his head. "Gwen has the strongest motive for everything that's happening. She wants that story."

Gwen stepped forward, positioning herself directly in front of Hollywood. "Holden or Helena could be paying you big bucks for information. For that matter, the money could be coming directly from Paul's estate."

"I wouldn't take blood money," Hollywood insisted, ramming his finger against his chest. "But you would. So would Holden or Helena."

So this could all come down to money. That didn't shock Jenna, but it sickened her to know that her daughter could be in danger simply because someone wanted to get rich.

Cal glanced at Jordan to make sure the area was still safe. He waited until Jordan nodded before he continued the conversation with Hollywood. "Any reason you didn't tell me yesterday that you'd had sex with a person of interest in this investigation?"

The frustration in Hollywood's expression went up a significant notch. His chest pumped with his harsh breaths. "Before you judge me, I think you should remind yourself why you're here. You slept with Jenna while she was in your protective custody."

Jenna wanted to set the record straight for Cal's sake, but he caught her hand and gave it a gentle warning squeeze.

"I can't trust either of you," Cal said to Hollywood and Gwen. "I don't care what your motives are. I want you to back off and leave Jenna and Sophie alone."

"You should be telling the Carrs this," Gwen pointed out.

"Maybe you'll do that for me." Cal didn't continue until Gwen looked him in the eye. "You can also tell them that Jenna, Sophie and I are leaving the estate within the hour. We're already packed and ready to go."

Jenna went still. Had Cal really planned that, or was this a ruse to get everyone off their trail?

"You think that's a wise move?" Hollywood asked.

"I think it's a *safe* move. And this time, I'll check and make sure there aren't any tracking devices on the vehicle we use."

Gwen turned and faced Jenna. Her expression wasn't as tense as Hollywood's, but emotion tightened the muscles in her jaw. "No matter where you go, the Carrs will find you."

"And you, too?"

Gwen shrugged and folded her arms over her chest. "I plan to write a story about Paul's murder."

"Then this meeting is over," Cal insisted. He put his hand on Hollywood's shoulder to get him moving out the door.

"I'm innocent," Hollywood declared. "But I don't expect you to trust me. Just hear this, I'll do whatever's necessary to clear my name."

"If you do that, I'll be overjoyed. But for right now, I don't want you anywhere near Jenna or Sophie. Got that?" It was an order, not a request.

Hollywood nodded and walked out. So did Gwen. Both went to their respective vehicles, but Jordan didn't return Hollywood's gun until the man had started his engine and was ready to leave. Jenna and Cal stood inside the gatehouse and watched the duo drive away.

"Are we really leaving the estate?" Jenna asked.

"No," he whispered. "But I want to make it look as if we are. Then I can continue to beef up security here, and we can stay put until all of this is resolved."

Cal's plan seemed like their best option. She didn't like the idea of traveling anywhere while her daughter was a target.

They walked out of the gatehouse and started for the estate. After the battle they'd just had with their visitors, Jenna suddenly had a strong need to check on Sophie.

"You think Hollywood and Gwen will believe we're leaving?" She checked over her shoulder to make sure they were gone. Jordan was keeping watch to make sure they didn't double back.

"Jordan's employee will drive out of here in a couple of minutes," Cal explained. He caught her arm and picked up the pace to get them to the porch. "He'll be using a vehicle with heavily tinted windows. As an extra pre-caution we won't use any of the house phones. They might be tapped, and I don't want anyone to know we're here. We can use the secure cell phone that Director Kowalski gave to me."

Jenna hoped that would be enough. And that Kowalski hadn't given Cal compromised equipment. After all, someone had managed to put those tracking devices on their cars.

"Get down!" she heard Jordan yell.

Jenna started to look back at him to see what had caused him to shout that, but Cal didn't give her a chance. He hooked his arm around her waist and dragged her between the flagstone porch steps and some shrubs.

Jordan dove into the gatehouse. His eyes were darting all around, looking for something.

But what?

Jenna didn't have to wait long for an answer.

"Salazar's on the grounds," Jordan shouted.

Chapter Twelve

If Salazar was on the grounds, he had come there for one reason: to get Sophie. If the assassin had to take out Jenna and Cal, that wouldn't matter. A man like Salazar wouldn't let anything get in the way of trying to accomplish his mission.

Later, after Cal had gotten Jenna out of this mess, he'd want to know just how Salazar had managed to get through what was supposed to be the secured perimeter of the estate. But for now, he had to focus on keeping Jenna and Sophie safe.

He lifted his head a little and assessed their situation. Jordan was in the doorway of the gatehouse, but he hadn't pinpointed Salazar's position. But someone had. Probably Jordan's assistant, Cody Guillory. The man had spotted Salazar and relayed that info through the communicator Jordan was wearing. Since Cal didn't know the exact location of Jordan's assistant, that meant Salazar could be anywhere.

Cal glanced at the front door. It was a good twenty feet away. It wasn't that far, but they'd literally be out in the open if he tried to get Jenna inside. Besides, it was locked and it would take a second or two to open it. That'd be time they were in Salazar's kill zone. Not a good option. At least if they stayed put, the stone steps would give them some protection.

Unless Salazar planned to launch explosives at them.

"Call Meggie," Cal said, handing Jenna his cell phone. "Make sure she's okay. Then tell her to set the alarm and move Sophie to the gun room."

He didn't risk looking at Jenna, though he knew that particular instruction would be a brutal reminder of the danger they were in. Jenna already knew, of course, but by now she probably had nightmarish images of Salazar breaking into the house.

With her voice trembling and her hands shaking, Jenna made the call. Cal shut out what she was saying and focused on their surroundings. He tried to anticipate how and where Salazar would launch an attack. There were more than a dozen possibilities. Salazar might even try to take out Jordan first.

A shot cracked through the air and landed in one of the porch pillars.

Cal automatically shoved Jenna farther down just in time. The next shot landed even lower. It sliced through the flagstone step just above their heads. Salazar had gone right for them. Cal prayed that Meggie had managed to set that alarm and get Sophie into the gun room.

The third shot took a path identical to the second. So did the fourth. Each bullet chipped away at the flagstone and sent jagged chunks of the rock flying right at them. Hell. Maybe staying put hadn't been such a good idea after all. Now they were trapped in a storm of shrapnel.

Cal pushed aside the feeling that he'd just made a fatal mistake and concentrated on the direction of the shots. Salazar was using a long-range assault rifle from somewhere out in the formal garden amid the manicured shrubs and white marble statues. There were at least a hundred places to hide, and nearly every one of them would be out of range for Cal's handgun.

Another shot sent a slice of the flagstone

ripping across Cal's shirtsleeve. Since the rock could do almost as much damage as a bullet, he crawled over Jenna, sheltering her as much as he could. She was shaking, but she also had a firm grip on the gun he'd given her earlier. Yes, she was scared, but she was also ready to fight back if she got the chance. This wasn't the same woman he'd rescued in Monte de Leon. But then, the stakes were higher for her now.

She had Sophie to protect.

His only hope was that Salazar would move closer so that Cal would have a better shot or Jordan could get to him. One of them had to stop the man before he escalated the attack.

There was another spray of bullets, and even though Cal sheltered his eyes from the flying debris, he figured Salazar had succeeded in tearing away more layers of their meager protection. Cal couldn't wait to see if Salazar was going to move. He had to do something to slow the man down.

Cal levered himself up just slightly and zoomed in on a row of hedges that stretched between two marble statues. He fired a shot in that direction.

A shot came right back at Cal, causing him to dip even lower. From the gatehouse,

Jordan fired a round. He was as far out of range as Cal. But between the two of them, they might manage to throw Salazar off his own deadly aimed shots. Not likely, though. Plus, they couldn't just randomly keep firing or they'd run out of ammunition.

But there was a trump card in all of this. Jordan's assistant. Maybe Cody Guillory was working his way toward Salazar so he could take him out.

The shots continued, the sound blasting through the chilly air and tainting it with the smells of gunpowder, sulfur and smoke. The constant stream of bullets caused his ears to ring. But the ringing wasn't so loud that he didn't hear a sound that sent his stomach to his knees.

The alarm. Someone had tripped the security system.

Which meant someone had broken in. Salazar or his henchman. Salazar normally worked alone, but this time he obviously hadn't come solo. There must be two of them. One firing at them while the other broke inside. Both trained to the hilt to make sure this mission was a success.

Jenna tried to get up. Cal shoved her right back down. And not a moment too soon. A barrage of bullets came their way. Each of the shots sprayed them with bits of rock and caused their adrenaline levels to spike. As long as those shots continued, it'd be suicide to try to get to the door and into the house.

But that was exactly what Cal had to do.

Meggie and Sophie were probably locked in the gun room, but that didn't mean Salazar wouldn't try to get to them. Hell, he might even succeed. And then he could kidnap Sophie and sneak her out, all while they were trapped out front dodging bullets.

"I'm going in," Cal told her. "Stay put."

She was shaking her head before he even finished. "No. I need to get to Sophie."

"I'll get to her. You need to stay here."

It was a risk. A huge one. Salazar could have planned it this way. Divide and conquer. Still, what was left of the steps was better protection than dragging Jenna onto the porch. Cal took a deep breath and got ready to scramble up the steps.

But just like that, the shots stopped.

And that terrified him.

Had the shooter left his position so he, too, could get into the house?

"Cover me," Cal shouted to Jordan, knowing that the man couldn't do a lot in that department. Still, fired shots might cause a distraction in case the gunman was still out there and ready to strike.

Cal didn't bother with the house keys. That would take too long. He'd have to bash in the door and hope that it gave way with only one well-positioned kick.

Jordan started firing shots. Thick blasts that he aimed at the hedges and other parts of the formal garden.

"I'm going with you," Jenna insisted.

Cal wanted to throttle her. Or at least yell for her to stay put. But he couldn't take the time to do either. Jordan's firepower wouldn't last. Each shot meant he was using up precious resources.

"Now," Cal ordered since it seemed as if he would have a partner for this ordeal.

He climbed over the steps, making sure that Jenna stayed to his side so that she wouldn't be in the direct line of fire from anyone who might still be in those hedges. Cal reached the door and gave it a fierce kick. It flew open, thank God. That was a start. But it occurred to Cal that he could be taking Jenna out of the frying pan and directly into the fire.

Cal shoved her against the foyer wall and placed himself in front of her. He disarmed the security system to stop the alarm. Then he paused, listening. He tried to pick through the sounds of Jordan's shots and the house. And he heard something he didn't want to hear.

Footsteps.

Someone was running through the house. Hopefully Meggie was in the gun room. The obvious answer was Salazar.

"I have to get to Sophie," Jenna said on a rise of breath. She broke away from him and started to run right toward those footsteps.

JENNA BARELY MADE IT a step before Cal latched on to her and dragged her behind him.

Her first instinct was to fight him off. To run. So she could get to her baby to make sure she was safe. But Cal held on tight, refusing to let her go.

"Shhh," he warned, turning his head in the direction of those menacing footsteps.

Salazar had managed to break through security, and he was probably inside, going after Sophie.

Cal started moving quietly, but quickly. He kept her behind him as he made his way down the east corridor toward the gun room.

"Keep watch behind us," he whispered.

Jenna automatically gripped her gun

tighter, and slid her index finger in front of the trigger. It was ironic that just an hour earlier she'd gotten her first shooting lesson, and now she might have to use the skills that Cal had taught her. She hoped she remembered everything because this wouldn't be a target with the outline of a man. It would be a professional assassin.

That was just the reminder she needed. It didn't matter if she had no experience with a firearm. She'd do whatever was necessary to protect Sophie.

Cal's footsteps hardly made a sound on the hardwood floors of the corridor. Jenna tried to keep her steps light as well, but she knew she was breathing too hard. And her heartbeat was pounding so loudly that she was worried someone might be able to hear it. Though with Cal bashing down the door, the element of surprise was gone. Still, she didn't want Salazar to be able to pinpoint their exact location.

Just in case, she lifted her gun so that she'd be ready to fire.

She and Cal moved together, but it seemed to take an eternity to reach the L-shaped turn in the corridor. Cal stopped then and peered around the corner.

"All clear," he mouthed.

No one was anywhere near the door to the gun room. Of course, that didn't mean that someone hadn't already gotten inside.

Her heart rate spiked, and she held her breath as they approached the room. The door was shut, and while keeping watch all around them, Cal reached down and tested the knob.

"It's locked," he whispered.

She released the breath she'd been holding, only to realize that Salazar could still have gotten inside and simply relocked the door.

Cal pressed the intercom positioned on the wall next to the door. "Meggie, is everything okay?" he whispered.

"Yes," the woman immediately answered.

Relief caused Jenna's knees to become weak. She had to press her left hand against the wall to steady herself. "Sophie's okay?"

"She's fine. What's going on?"

But there was no time to answer.

Movement at one end of the hall made Cal pivot in that direction. "Get down," he ordered her.

Jenna ducked and glanced in that direction. She saw the dark sleeve of what appeared to be a man's coat. Salazar.

Cal fired, the shot blistering through the corridor.

She didn't look to see what the outcome of that shot was because she saw something at the other end of the hall.

With her heart in her throat, she took aim. Waited. Prayed. She didn't have to wait long. A man peered around the corner. He had a gun and pointed it right at her.

Jenna didn't even allow herself time to think. This man wasn't getting anywhere near her daughter.

She squeezed the trigger and fired.

Chapter Thirteen

Cal forced Jenna to sit on the leather sofa of the family room.

He didn't have to exert much force. He just gently guided her off her feet. She wasn't trembling. Wasn't crying. But her blank stare and silence let him know that she was probably in shock.

Once the director was finished with the initial investigation and reports, Cal needed to talk her into getting some medical care. She'd already refused several times, but he'd keep trying.

Two men were dead.

Cal was responsible for one of those deaths. He'd taken out Salazar with two shots to the head. Jenna had neutralized Salazar's henchman. Her single shot had entered the man's chest. Death hadn't been immediate—he'd died while being transported to the hospital. Unfortunately, the man hadn't made any deathbed confessions.

Cal got up, went to a bar that was partly concealed behind a stained-glass cabinet door, and poured Jenna a shot of whiskey. "Drink this," he said, returning to the sofa to sit next to her.

As if operating on autopilot, she tasted it and grimaced, her eyes watering.

"Take another sip," he insisted.

She did and then finished off the shot. She set the glass on the coffee table and folded her hands in her lap. "Does killing someone ever get easier?" she asked.

"No."

He hated that this was a lesson she'd had to learn. What she'd done was necessary. But it would stay with her forever.

She glanced around the room as if seeing the activity for the first time. Director Kowalski was there near the doorway, talking to two FBI agents and a local sheriff. They were all lawmen with jurisdiction, but Kowalski was unofficially leading the show. This had international implications, and there were people who would want to keep that under wraps.

Jenna's eyes met his. The blankness was

fading. She was slowly coming to terms with what had happened, but once the full impact hit her, she'd fall apart.

But Cal would be right there to catch her.

"Sophie," she said, sounding alarmed. She started to get up. "I need to check on her again."

Cal caught her. "I just checked on her a few minutes ago. Sophie's fine. Jordan's still with her and Meggie in the nursery. Even though there's no way she'd remember any of this, I didn't want her to be out here right now."

His attention drifted in the direction of the corridor where federal agents were cleaning up the crime scene.

Cal didn't want Sophie anywhere around that.

Jenna nodded. "Thank you."

He saw it then. Jenna's bottom lip trembled. He slid his arm around her and hoped this preliminary investigation would end soon so her meltdown wouldn't happen in front of the others.

"You did a good thing in that corridor," Cal reminded her. "You did what you needed to do."

The corner of her mouth lifted, but there was no humor in her smile. "You gave me a good shooting lesson."

Yeah. But he'd given her that lesson with the hopes that she'd never have to use a gun.

Kowalski stepped away from the others and walked toward them. He stopped, studied Jenna and looked at Cal. "Is she okay?"

"Yes," Jenna answered at the exact moment that Cal answered, "No."

The director just nodded. "I don't want any of this in a local report," he instructed Cal. "The sheriff has agreed to back off. No questions. He'll let us do our jobs, and the FBI will file the official paperwork after I've read through and approved it."

"I'll need to give a statement," Jenna concluded. Emotion was making her voice tremble.

"It can wait," Kowalski assured her. "But I don't want you talking to anyone about this, understand?"

"Yes." This would be sanitized and classified. No one outside this estate would learn that an international assassin had entered the country to go after a Texas heiress. The hush-up would protect Jenna and Sophie from the press, but it wouldn't help Jenna deal with the aftermath.

"Any idea how Salazar got onto the grounds?" Cal wanted to know.

"It appears he was here before your friend Jordan Taylor even put his security measures into place. There's evidence that Salazar was waiting in one of the storage buildings on the property."

Smart move. That meant Salazar had used the tracking device on Jenna's car to follow them to the estate, and he'd hidden out for a full day, waiting for the right time to strike. But why hadn't Salazar attacked earlier, when he and Jenna were outside meeting with the others? The only answer that Cal could come up with was that he had wanted as few witnesses as possible when he went after Sophie.

"Salazar and his accomplice broke in through French doors in one of the guest suites," Kowalski continued. "We believe the plan was to locate the child, kill anyone they encountered and then escape."

Jenna pressed her fingertips to her mouth, but Cal could still hear the soft sob. He tightened his grip on her, and it didn't go unnoticed. Kowalski flexed his eyebrows in a disapproving gesture.

Cal ignored him. "What about all the rest? Any idea who hired Salazar or if Hollywood had any part in this?"

The director shook his head. "There's no

evidence to indicate Agent Lynch is guilty of anything. He might have been set up."

That's what Hollywood was claiming, and it might be true. Still, Cal wasn't about to declare anyone's innocence just yet. "Who was paying Salazar?"

"The money was coming from Paul's estate, but his attorney will almost certainly say that he was unaware the payment was going to a hired killer."

"He might not have known," Cal mumbled.

Kowalski shrugged. "The ISA will deal with the attorney. But the good news is that Ms. Laniere and her child seem to be out of danger."

Jenna looked at the director. Then at Cal. He saw new concern in her eyes.

"I'm not leaving," Cal assured her.

That got him another flexed-eyebrow reaction from the director. "Tie things up around here," Kowalski ordered. "I want you back at headquarters tomorrow."

Cal got to his feet. "I'd like to take some personal time off."

"I can't approve that. Tomorrow, the promotion list should be arriving in my office. You'll know then if you've gotten the deputy director job." Kowalski's announcement seemed a little like a threat.

Choose between Jenna and the job.

"I'm sorry," Jenna whispered. She stood, too, and this time moved Cal's hand away when he tried to catch her. "I'm going to check on Sophie."

No. She was going to fall apart.

"I'll be at headquarters tomorrow," Cal assured the director. "But I'm still requesting a personal leave of absence." Without waiting to see if Kowalski had anything else to mandate, Cal went after Jenna.

She was moving pretty fast down the corridor, but he easily caught up with her. She didn't say anything. Didn't have to. He figured she was already trying to figure out how she was going to cope without him there.

Cal was trying to figure out the same thing.

Jordan stood in the doorway of the nursery. His gun wasn't drawn, but it was tucked away in a shoulder holster. "Everything okay?" he wanted to know.

Jenna maneuvered past him and went straight to her daughter. Sophie was awake and making cooing sounds as Meggie played peekaboo with her. Jenna scooped up the little girl in her arms and held on.

"The director and all the law enforcement guys will be leaving within an hour or two,"

Cal informed Jordan. He didn't go closer to Jenna. He stood back and watched as she held Sophie. "The threat might be over, but I'd like you to stay around for a while."

Jordan followed Cal's gaze to Jenna. "Is this job official?"

"No. Personal."

Jordan's attention snapped back to Cal. "You? Personal?"

"It happens."

Jordan didn't look as if he believed that. He shrugged. "I can give you two days. After that, it'll just be Cody. But he's good. I trained him myself."

Cal nodded his thanks. Hopefully, two days would be enough to tie up those loose ends the director had mentioned. Now if Cal could just figure out how to do that.

"Is she willing to take a sedative?" Jordan asked, tipping his head to Jenna.

Cal didn't have to guess why Jordan had asked that. He could see Jenna's hand shaking. "Probably not." Even though it would make the next few hours easier.

"My advice?" Jordan said. "Liberal shots of good scotch, a hot bath and some sleep."

All good ideas. Cal wondered if Jenna would cooperate with any of them. But when she began to shake even harder, she must have understood that merely holding her baby wasn't going to make this all go away.

Cal went to her and took Sophie. The little girl looked at him as if she didn't know if she should cry or smile. She settled for a big, toothless grin, which Cal realized made him feel a whole lot better. Maybe he'd been wrong about the effects of holding her. He kissed her cheek, got another smile and then handed her to Meggie.

"See to Jenna," Meggie whispered, obviously concerned about her employer.

Cal was concerned, too. He looped his arm around Jenna's waist and led her out of the nursery. She didn't protest, and walked side by side with him to her suite.

"It's stupid to feel like this," Jenna mumbled. "That man would have killed us if I hadn't shot him."

Her words were true. But he doubted the truth would make it easier for her to accept.

"You're so calm," she pointed out, stepping inside the room. It was the first time he'd been in her suite. Like the rest of the house, it was big and decorated in soothing shades of cream and pale blue. He wasn't counting on those colors to soothe her, though. It'd take more than interior decorating to do that.

Cal shut the door. "I'm not calm," he assured her.

"You look calm." Her voice broke on the last word. Cal waited for tears, but she didn't cry. Instead, she moved closer to him. "My baby's safe," she muttered. "We're safe. Salazar is dead. And you'll be leaving soon to go back to headquarters."

He shook his head, not knowing what to say. Yes, he probably would leave for that morning meeting with Kowalski. He opened his mouth to answer, to try to reassure her that he'd be back. But Jenna pressed her hand over his lips.

"Don't make promises you can't keep," she said. She tilted her head to the side and stared at him. "I'm going to do something really stupid. Something we'll regret."

Jenna slid her hand away, and her mouth came to his, kissing him.

The shock of that kiss roared through Cal for just a split second. Then the shock was replaced with the jolt of something stronger—pleasure. His body automatically went from comfort and protect mode to something primal. Something that had him taking hold of her and dragging her to him.

He made that kiss his own, claiming her mouth. Taking her. Demanding all that she had to give.

His hands were on her. Her hands, on him. Their embrace was hungry, frenzied. Both of them wanted more and were taking it.

And then he got another jolt…of reality.

Sex wasn't a good idea right now. Not with Jenna on the verge of a meltdown.

He forced himself to stop.

With her breath gusting, Jenna looked at him. "No," she said. She came at him again. There was another fast and furious kiss. It was hard, brutal and in some ways punishing. It was also what she needed.

Cal felt the weariness drain from her. Or maybe she was merely channeling all her emotions into this dangerous energy. She shoved him against the door, fusing her mouth to his, her hands going after his shirt.

Part of him wanted to get naked and take her right there. But only one of them could get crazy at the same time. Since Jenna had latched on to that role, Cal knew he had to be the voice of reason.

But then her breasts ground against his chest. And her sex pressed against his.

Oh, yeah.

That put a dent in any rational thought.

Still, somehow, he managed to catch her arms and hold her at bay so he could voice a little of the reasoning he was desperately trying to hang on to.

"You're not ready for this," he insisted.

"I'm ready." There wasn't any doubt in her tone. Her eyes. Her body.

She shook off his grip, took his hand and slid it down into the waist of her loose jeans. Into her panties. She was wet and hot.

Oh, mercy.

Then she ran her own palm over the very noticeable bulge in his pants. "You're ready."

"No condom," he ground out.

Jenna's eyes widened, and she darted away from him. She ran to a dresser on the other side of the room, and frantically, began searching through the drawers. Several moments later, she produced a foil-wrapped condom.

Cal didn't give her even a second to celebrate. He locked the door and hurried to her. He grabbed the condom, and in the same motion, he grabbed her. He kissed her and backed her against the dresser.

The kiss continued as they fought with each other's clothes. He got off her top, and while he wanted to sample her breasts—man, she was beautiful—his body was urging him in a different direction.

With her butt balancing her against the edge of the dresser, he stripped off her jeans. And her white lace panties. By then, she was all over him. Her mouth, hungry on his neck. Her hands fighting with his zipper. She won that fight, and took him into her hands.

Cal didn't breathe for a couple of seconds. He didn't care if he ever breathed again. He just wanted one thing.

Jenna.

He opened the condom and put it on. "This is your last chance to say no."

She looked at him as if he were crazy. Maybe he was. Maybe they both were. Jenna hoisted herself up on the edge of the dresser.

"I'm saying yes," she assured him.

To prove it, she hooked her legs around him, thrust him forward and he slid hot and deep into her.

He stilled a moment. To give her time to adjust to the primal invasion of her tight body. He watched her face, looking for any sign that she might be in pain.

Angling her body back, she slid forward, giving him a delicious view of her breasts and their joined bodies.

She wasn't the pampered heiress now. She was his lover. Funny, he hadn't thought she would be this bold, but he appreciated it on many, many levels.

"Don't treat me like glass," she whispered.

"No intention of that," he promised.

He caught her hair and pulled her head back slightly to expose her neck. He kissed there and drove into her.

Hard.

Fast.

Deep.

Her reaction was priceless. Something he'd remember for the rest of his life. She grabbed him by his hair and jerked his head forward, forcing eye contact. And with her hand fisted in his hair, she moved, meeting him thrust for thrust.

Their mouths were so close he could almost taste her, but she was just out of reach. Instead, her breath caressed his mouth while her legs tightened around him.

Their frantic rhythm created the friction that fueled her need. It became unbearable. She closed around him, her body shuddering. The unbearable need went to a whole different level.

She sighed his name. "Cal." Jenna repeated

it like some ancient plea for him to join her in that whirl of primitive pleasure.

Cal leaned in, pushing into her one last time. He kissed her and surrendered.

Even with his pulse crashing in his ears and head, he heard the one word that came from his mouth.

Jenna.

SHE WAS HALF-NAKED on a dresser. Out of breath, sweaty and exhausted. And coming down from one of the worst days of her life. Yet it'd been a long time since Jenna had felt this good. She bit back a laugh. Cal would think she was losing her mind.

And maybe she was.

This shouldn't have happened. Being with Cal like this only made her feel closer to him. It only made her want him more. But that wasn't in their future. She was well on her way to a broken heart.

"Hell," Cal mumbled. "We had sex on the dresser."

He blinked as if trying to focus and huffed out short jolts of breath. He was sweaty, too. And hot. Just looking at him made her want him all over again.

"You don't think I'm the sex-on-the-dresser

type?" she asked, trying to keep things light for her own sanity. She couldn't lose it. Not now. Because soon, very soon, Cal would begin to regret this, and she didn't want her fragile mental state playing into his guilt.

With his breath still gusting, he leaned in and brushed a kiss on her mouth. It went straight through her, warm and liquid. "I thought you'd prefer sex on silk sheets," he mumbled.

Still reeling a little from that kiss, she ran her tongue over her bottom lip and tasted him there. "No silk sheets required."

Just you. Thankfully she kept that thought to herself.

He withdrew from her, gently. Unlike the firestorm that'd happened only moments earlier. Cal helped her to her feet, made sure she was steady and then he went into the adjacent bathroom.

Jenna took a moment to compose herself and remembered there were a lot of people still in her house. FBI, Kowalski, the sheriff. She started to have some doubts of her own. She should be focusing on the shootings.

But the shootings could wait. Right now she needed to put on a good front for Cal, spend some time with her daughter and try to figure out where to go from here.

Her old instincts urged her to run. To try to escape emotions she didn't want to face. But running would only be a temporary solution. She looked up and could almost hear her father saying that to her. Funny that it would sink in now when her life was at its messiest.

She needed to stay put, and concentrate on getting Helena, Holden and Gwen out of her life. While she was at it, she also needed to hold her daughter. Oh, and she had to figure out how to nurse her soon-to-be-broken heart.

With her list complete, she started to get dressed. She was still stepping into her jeans when Cal returned.

He looked at her with those scorching blue eyes and had her going all hot again. Jenna pushed aside her desire, reminding her body that it'd just gotten lucky. That wasn't going to happen again any time soon.

"You okay?" he asked.

Jenna nodded and was surprised to realize that it was true. She wasn't a basket case. She wasn't on the verge of sobbing. She felt strong because she had been able to help protect her baby.

He shoved his hands into his pockets.

"When things settle down, you might want to see a therapist. There are a lot of emotions that might come up later."

She nodded again and put her own hands in her pockets. "Now that Salazar is dead, it's time to clear up Sophie's paternity with your director."

He looked down at the floor. "Best not to do that. We don't know who hired Salazar, and until we do, nothing is clear."

Confused, Jenna shook her head. "But certainly it doesn't matter if everyone knows that Sophie is Paul's biological child."

"It might matter." He paused and met her gaze. "Gwen was having an affair with Paul. Helena, too. Either could be jealous and want to get back at you. Either could have sent Salazar to take Sophie because they feel they should be the one who's raising her."

Oh, God. She hadn't even considered that, and she couldn't dismiss it. Both Helena and Gwen hadn't been on the up-and-up about much of anything.

"Holden could be a problem, too," Cal continued. "Paul might have told him to take any child that you and he might have produced. The child would be Paul's heir, and Holden would like nothing more than to control the heir to a vast estate."

Her chest tightened. It felt as if someone had clamped a fist around her heart. "So Sophie could still be in danger?"

"It's possible." He took his hands from his pocket and brought out his phone.

Alarmed, she crossed the room to him. "What are you going to do?"

"Something I should have done already." He scrolled through the numbers stored in his phone, located one and hit the call button. "Director Kowalski," he said a moment later. "Are you still at the estate? I need to speak to you."

Jenna shook her head. "No," she mouthed.

But Cal didn't listen to her. He stepped away, turning his back to her. "I'll meet you in the living room in a few minutes." He hung up and walked out the door.

She caught his arm. "What are you going to say to him?"

"I'll tell him that I lied. That Sophie is my daughter. I want to start the paperwork to have Sophie legally declared my child. I'll do that when I get to headquarters in the morning."

Oh, mercy. He was talking about legally becoming a father. Cal would make an amazing dad. She could tell that from the way he handled her daughter. But this arrangement would cost him that promotion.

"You don't have to do this," Jenna insisted. "We'll find another way to make sure she's safe."

"There is no other way." He caught her shoulders and looked her straight in the eye. "This is your chance at having a normal life. This way you won't always be looking over your shoulder."

"But what about you? What about your career?"

A muscle flickered in his jaw, and she saw anger flare in his eyes. "Do you really think I'm the kind of man who would endanger a child for the sake of a promotion?" He sounded disappointed. "I'm going to do this, Jenna, with or without your approval."

And with that, he walked out.

Chapter Fourteen

Cal hadn't expected Kowalski's ultimatum.

But he should have. He should have known the director wasn't going to let him have a happy ending.

He stood at the door and watched Kowalski, the FBI agents and the sheriff drive away. Now that the sun had set, a chilly fog had moved in, and the cars' brakes lights flashed in the darkness like eerie warnings. Jordan was there to shut the gate behind them. He gave Cal a thumbs-up before heading in the direction of the garden. He was probably going to give his assistant some further instructions about security.

The security measures wouldn't be suspended simply because everyone else had left the estate. Jordan, or one of his employees, would stay on as long as necessary. Of course, Cal still had to get out the word, or rather the lie, that Sophie was his child. Once that was done, he would deal with the ultimatum Kowalski had delivered just minutes before he left.

Cal closed the front door, locked it and reset the security system before he went in search of Jenna. He dreaded this meeting with her almost as much as he'd dreaded the one he'd just had with Kowalski. He felt both numb and drained.

He'd killed a man today. It was never easy even when necessary as this one had been. But his difficulty dealing with the death was minor compared to Jenna's. She'd killed a man, too. Her first. In fact, the first time she'd ever fired a gun at another human being.

This would stay with her forever.

Maybe that's why sex had followed. That was a surefire way to burn off some of her high-anxiety adrenaline. Cal shook his head.

It had felt real. And that was a big problem.

He'd compounded it by arguing with Kowalski. The conversation had been necessary, and Cal didn't regret it. But that wouldn't make his chat with Jenna any easier. She needed to know what the director had ordered him to do. And then he somehow had to convince her, and himself, that he could follow through and do what had to be done.

Cal found her in the kitchen. Meggie was at the stove adding some seasoning to a great-smelling pot roast. Jenna was seated at the table feeding Sophie a bottle. Jenna looked as tired and troubled as he felt.

Unlike Sophie.

When the little girl spotted him, she turned her head so that the bottle came out of her mouth. And she smiled at him.

He smiled right back.

Weariness drained right out of him. He wasn't sure how someone so small could create dozens of little daily miracles.

Sophie squirmed, pushing the bottle away, and made some cooing sounds.

"I interrupted her dinner," he commented. Cal sat in the chair next to them.

"She was just about finished, anyway." Jenna's tone was tentative, and she studied him, searching his eyes for any indication of how the conversation with Kowalski had gone.

Sophie reached for him, and Cal took her into his arms. He got yet another smile. It filled him with warmth and it broke his heart.

What the devil was he going to do?

How could he give up this child that'd already grabbed hold of him?

"Something's wrong," Jenna said. She

touched his arm gently, drawing his attention back to her.

"Uh, I need to check on something," Meggie suddenly announced. She adjusted the temperature on the pot roast and scooted out of the kitchen. She was a perceptive woman.

"Well?" Jenna prompted.

Best to start from the beginning. "Kowalski didn't buy my story about being Sophie's father. The ISA has retrieved one of Sophie's pacifiers from your apartment in Willow Ridge and compared the DNA to mine. Kowalski knows I'm not a match. It's just a matter of time before he learns that Paul is."

"I see." She repeated it and drew back her hand, letting it settle into her lap. "Well, that's good for you. He doesn't still think you slept with me, does he?"

"No." Cal brushed a kiss on Sophie's cheek. "And Kowalski will keep the DNA test a secret."

He hoped. Kowalski had promised that, anyway.

"But?" Jenna questioned.

"I told him I still wanted to do the paperwork to have Sophie declared my child. I want the DNA test doctored. I want anyone associated with Paul to believe she's mine so they'll back off."

Jenna fastened her attention on him. "There's more, isn't there?"

Cal cleared his throat. "In the morning you'll go into temporary protective custody. Kowalski will leak the fake DNA results through official and unofficial channels, and you and Sophie will stay in protective custody until everyone is sure the danger has passed. He thinks it shouldn't be more than a month or two before the ISA finds out who's responsible for this mess and gets that person off the streets."

"The ISA?" she repeated after a long pause. "But you said your organization doesn't normally handle domestic situations."

"Sometimes they make exceptions."

"I see." Jenna paused again, studying him. Worry lines bunched up her forehead. "And what about you? How does all of this affect you?"

Cal took a deep breath. "Kowalski will tell the chief director the truth, that this is all part of a plan to guarantee your safety." Another deep breath. "In exchange for his guarantee of your safety, Kowalski wants me to extract myself from the situation."

Her eyes widened. "Extract?" she questioned. "What does that mean exactly?"

He'd rehearsed this part. "Kowalski thinks I've lost my objectivity with you and Sophie. He thinks I'll be a danger to both of you and myself if I stay." Cal choked back a groan. "It's standard procedure to extract an agent when there's even a hint of any conflict of interest."

Though nothing about this felt standard. Of course, Cal couldn't deny that he'd stepped way over a lot of lines when it came to Jenna.

Sophie batted him on the nose and put her mouth on his cheek as if giving him a kiss.

Cal took yet more deep breaths. "By doctoring the records and the DNA, Kowalski will be protecting you. But he wants me to swear that I won't see you or Sophie until there's no longer a threat to either of you."

Jenna went still. "But the threat might always be there."

Cal nodded and watched the pain of that creep into her eyes.

She quickly looked away. "Okay. This is good. It means you'll probably get your promotion. Sophie will be safe. And I'll get on with my life." Jenna stood, walked across the room and looked out the window. "So when do you leave?"

"Kowalski wanted me to leave immediately, but I told him I'd go in the morning when the ISA agents arrive."

She stood there, silent, with her back to him.

It was because of the sudden silence in the room that Cal had no trouble hearing a loud crash that came from outside the house.

He got to his feet, and while balancing Sophie, he took out his phone to call Jordan. But his phone rang first. Jordan's name and number appeared on the caller ID screen.

"Cal, we've got a problem," Jordan informed him. "Someone just broke though the front gate."

Before Cal could question him, there was another sound. One he definitely didn't want to hear.

Someone fired a shot.

JORDAN'S VOICE WAS LOUD enough that Jenna heard what he said. If she hadn't heard the crash, she might have wondered what the heck he was talking about. But there was no mistaking the noise of something tearing through the metal gates.

And then it sounded as if someone had fired a gun. It was too much to hope that the noise was from a car backfiring.

While Cal continued to talk with Jordan, Jenna reached for Sophie, and Cal reached for his gun.

"Try to contain the situation as planned," Cal instructed Jordan. "I'll take care of things here."

He shoved his phone back into his pocket and turned to her to give her instructions. But Meggie interrupted them when she came running back into the kitchen.

The woman was as pale as a ghost. "I saw out the window," she said, her voice filled with fear. "A Hummer rammed through the gate. Some guys wearing ski masks got out, and one of them shot the man that came here with Jordan Taylor."

Jenna's gaze went to Cal's, and with one look he confirmed that was true. "How many men got out of the Hummer?" Cal asked Meggie. He sounded calm, but he gripped Jenna's arm and got them moving out of the kitchen.

"Four, I think," Meggie answered. "Maybe more. All of them had guns."

Four armed men. Jenna knew what they were after: Sophie. Salazar had failed, but someone else had been sent to do the job.

There was another shot. Then another. Thick blasts that sounded like those that had come from Salazar. Someone was shooting a rifle at Jordan. He was out there and under attack. It wouldn't be long, maybe seconds, before the gunman got past Jordan and into the house.

Cal headed for the gun room. There was no escape route there, and Jenna knew what he planned to do. Cal wanted Meggie, Sophie and her to be shut away behind bulletproof walls while he tried to protect them. But it was four against two. Not good odds especially when her daughter's safety was at stake.

"I'm going to help you," Jenna insisted. She handed Sophie to Meggie and motioned for the woman to go deep into the gun room. Jenna grabbed two of the automatic weapons from the case.

"I need to make sure you're safe," Cal countered. Though he was busy grabbing weapons and ammunition, he managed to toss her a firm scowl. "You're staying here."

Outside, there was a flurry of gunfire.

Jenna shook her head. "You need backup." She wasn't going to hide while Cal risked his life. "If they get past Jordan and you, the gunmen will figure out a way to get into that room. They might even have explosives. Sophie could be hurt."

He shoved some magazines of ammo into

his pockets, then stopped and stared at her. "I can't risk you getting hurt."

She looked him straight in the eye. "I can't risk Sophie's life. I'm going, Cal. And you can't stop me."

He cursed, glanced around the room at Sophie and Meggie. If her daughter was aware of the danger, it certainly didn't show. Sophie was cooing.

"Stay behind me," Cal snarled to Jenna.

She didn't exactly celebrate the concession, though she knew for him, it was a huge one. Jenna looked at Sophie one last time.

"Lock the door from the inside and stay in the center of the room, away from the walls," Cal instructed Meggie. Then he shut it.

Jenna didn't have time to dwell on her decision because Cal started toward the end of the corridor.

"What's the plan?" she asked.

"We go to the front of the house where the intruders are, but we stay inside until we hear from Jordan. He'll try to secure the perimeter."

"Alone? Against four gunmen?" Mercy, that didn't sound like much of a plan at all. It sounded like suicide.

"Jordan knows how to handle situations

like these." But Cal didn't sound nearly as convinced as his words would pretend.

Jenna didn't doubt Jordan's capabilities, either. But he was outnumbered and out-gunned.

"Jordan knows I have to stay inside," Cal added. He headed straight for the front of the house, and Jenna was right behind him. "I'm the last line of defense against anyone trying to get to Sophie."

However, they only made it a few steps before there was another crash. It sounded as if someone had bashed the front door in.

Oh, God.

Jenna's heart began to pound as alarms pierced through the house. The security system had been tripped.

Which meant someone was inside.

Chapter Fifteen

This could not be happening.

He and Jenna had already survived one attack from Salazar, and now they were facing another.

He pulled Jenna inside one of the middle rooms off the corridor and listened for any sign that it was Jordan who'd burst through that door. But he knew Jordan would have identified himself. Jordan was a pro and wouldn't have risked being shot by friendly fire.

And that meant it was the gunmen who'd bashed their way in.

So Jenna and he had moved from being backups to primary defense. He sure as hell hadn't wanted her to be in this position, but there was no other choice. They might need both of them to stop the gunmen from getting to Sophie. The gun room was much safer than the rest of the house, but it wasn't foolproof.

If the gunmen eliminated them, they'd eventually find their way to Sophie.

Cal was prepared to die to make sure that didn't happen.

He heard movement coming from the foyer. He also heard Jenna's breathing and then her soft mumbling. She was mouthing something, probably meant to keep her calm.

It wouldn't work.

Not with her child at risk. Cal was trained to deal with these types of intense scenarios, and even with all that training, he had to battle his emotions.

And that made this situation even more dangerous.

He forced himself to think like an operative. He was well equipped to deal with circumstances just like this. So what would happen next? What did he need to do to make this survivable?

At least four armed men had invaded the house. Even if they knew the layout, they wouldn't know where Sophie was. Which meant they'd have to go searching for their prize. They wouldn't do that as a group.

Too risky.

Too much noise.

They'd split up in pairs with one pair

taking the west corridor. The other would take the east, which was closer to the gun room. The pairs would almost certainly search the entire place, going from room to room. That meant at least two would soon be coming their way. The other two wouldn't be that far behind.

Cal eased out of the doorway so he could see the west corridor entrance. Even though he didn't hear anything, he detected some movement and saw a man in a blue ski mask peer around the corner, so, "Blue" was already in place and ready to strike.

Cal didn't make any sudden moves. For now, he needed to stay put and stay quiet, all the while hoping the doorjamb would conceal him.

A moment later, "Blue" and his partner quietly stepped into the corridor. "Blue" ducked into a room to search it, and the other kept watch.

Cal was going to have to do this the hard way. He didn't want to start a gun battle in the very hallway of the gun room, but he didn't have a choice. He'd have to take out the guy standing guard, and the moment he did that, it would put his partner and the other pair of gunmen on alert. Of course, they already knew he was in the house. They already knew he was trained to kill.

The question was: how good were they?

And the answer to that depended on who had hired them.

If it was Hollywood, well, Cal didn't want to think about how bad this could get. Hollywood had as much training as he did. They'd be an equal match. And God knows how this would end.

Cal didn't want to risk giving away his position, so he hoped that Jenna would stay put and not make any sounds. He got his primary gun ready, and without hesitating, he leaned out just far enough to get a clean shot.

The one standing guard saw him right away as Cal had expected. And he turned his gun on Cal. But it was a split second too late. Cal fired first. He didn't want to take any chance that this guy would survive and continue to be a threat, so he went with three shots, two to the head, one to the chest.

The gunman fell dead to the floor.

Jenna's breathing kicked up a notch, and he was sure she was shaking. He couldn't take the time to assure her that they'd get out of this alive. Because they might not. Those first shots were the only easy ones he would get. Everything else would be riskier.

Cal volleyed his attention between the room being searched and the other end of corridor. He needed help, and as much as he hated it, it would have to come from Jenna.

He angled himself in the doorway so that he was partly behind the cover of the door frame. "Watch," he instructed Jenna in a whisper. "Let me know when the gunmen come around the corner."

It was just a matter of time.

Cal's only hope was to take care of the "Blue" who was still in the room, and then start making his way toward the other pair. To do that, Jenna and he would have to use the rooms as cover. And then they'd have to pray that the second pair didn't backtrack and take the same path of their comrades. Cal didn't want them to be ambushed.

And there was one more massive problem.

While he watched for "Blue" to make an appearance from the room, Cal thought through the simple floor plan he'd seen on the security panel door. The east and west corridors flanked the center of the house, but there was at least one point of entry that the pair in the west hall could use to get to the side of the house where he and Jenna were.

The family room.

It could be accessed from either hall.

And if the pair used it, that meant they'd be making an appearance two rooms down on the right. He hoped that was the only point where that could happen. Of course, the floor plan on the security panel could have been incomplete.

But he couldn't make a plan based on what he didn't know. The most strategic place for Jenna and him to be was in that family room. That way they could guard the corridor and guard against an ambush. First, though, he had to neutralize "Blue."

There was still no movement near the dead gunman's body. No sound of communication, either. Cal couldn't wait too long or all three would converge on them at once. But neither could he storm the room. Too risky. He had to stay alive and uninjured so he could get Jenna, Meggie and Sophie out of this.

"Go back inside," he instructed Jenna in as soft a whisper as he could manage. "Move to your right and aim at the room where 'Blue' is. Fire a shot through the wall and then get down immediately."

She didn't question him. Jenna gave a

shaky nod and hurried to get into position. Cal kept watch, dividing his attention among "Blue's" position, the family room and the other end of the corridor.

Cal didn't risk looking at Jenna, but there was no way he could miss hearing her shot. The blast ripped through the wall and tore through the edge of the door frame of the other room.

Perfect.

It was exactly where Cal wanted it to go. And Jenna did exactly as he'd asked. He heard her drop to the floor.

Cal didn't have to wait long for a response. "Blue" returned fire almost immediately, and Cal saw a pair of bullets slam into the wall behind them. He calculated the angle of the shots, aimed and fired two shots of his own.

There was a groan of pain. Followed by a thud.

Even though he knew his shots had been dead-on, Cal didn't count it as a success. "Blue" could be alive, waiting to attack them. Still, there was a better than fifty-fifty chance that Cal had managed to neutralize him.

"Let's go," Cal whispered to Jenna. He had to get moving toward the family room, and he couldn't leave her alone. As dangerous as it was for her to be with him and out in the open, it would be more dangerous for her to stay put and run into the gunmen.

Jenna hurried to the doorway and stood next to him. She had her weapon ready. He only hoped her aim continued to be as good as that last shot.

"We go out back to back," he said. "You cover that end." He tipped his head toward the dead guy and the room with the bullet holes in the wall. "When we get to the family room, I want you to get down."

Judging from her questioning glance, Jenna didn't approve. Tough. He didn't want to have to worry about her being in the line of fire, and he would have three possible kill zones to cover.

Cal took out a second automatic so he'd have a full magazine, and stepped into the hall. Out in the open. Jenna quickly joined him and put her back to his. He waited just a second to see if anyone was going to dart out and fire at them. But he didn't see or hear anything.

"Let's go," he whispered.

They got moving toward the family room. Cal didn't count the steps, but each one pounded in his head and ears as if marking time. He thought of Sophie. Of Jenna. Of the

high stakes that could have fatal consequences. But he pushed those thoughts aside
and focused on what he had to do.

When they reached the family room, he
stopped and peered around the doorway. The
room was empty.

Or at least it seemed to be.

The double doors that led to the east
corridor were shut. That was good. If they'd
been open, the gunmen on that side of the
house would have heard them. Cal was
counting on those closed doors to act as a
buffer. And a warning. Because when the
pair opened them to search the room, Cal
would hear it and would be able to shoot at
least one of them.

"Check the furniture," Cal told her. "Make
sure we have this room to ourselves."

She moved around him while he tried to
keep watch in all directions. But Jenna had
barely taken a step when there was a sound.

Cal braced himself for someone to bash
through the doors. Or for one or more of the
gunmen to appear in the corridor. But the
sound hadn't come from those places.

It'd come from above.

He glanced up and then heard something
else. Hurried footsteps. He spotted a lone

gunman as he rounded the corner of the east corridor. Cal turned to take him out.

"Check the ceiling," Cal told Jenna as he fired at the man. But the man ducked into a room, evading the shot.

Cal made his own check of the ceiling then. Just a glance. The next sound was even louder. Maybe someone moving around in the attic.

He didn't have to wait long for an answer.

Two things happened simultaneously. The gunman who'd just ducked into the room across the hall darted out again. And there was a crash from above. Cal hadn't noticed the concealed attic door on the ceiling. It'd blended in with the decorative white tin tiles. But he noticed it now.

THE ATTIC DOOR flew back, and shots rang out from above them.

Cal shouted for her to get down, but Jenna was already diving behind an oversize leather sofa. From the moment she saw that attic door open, she knew what was about to come.

An ambush.

At least one of the gunmen had accessed the attic, and now she and Cal were under attack.

She fired at the shooter in the attic and missed. He ducked back out of sight. She couldn't see even his shadow amid the pitch-darkness of the attic.

But shots continued to rain down through the ceiling. That alone would have sent her adrenaline out of control, but then she thought of Sophie.

Oh, God.

Was the ceiling in the gun room bulletproof?

She couldn't remember her father saying for certain, but she had to pray that it was. She hoped there was no attic access in there. But just in case, they needed to take care of this situation so they could make sure that Sophie and Meggie were all right.

Cal fired, causing her attention to snap his way. He wasn't aiming at the ceiling, but rather at someone in the east end of the hall. Mercy. They were under attack from two different sides.

Dividing her focus between Cal and the ceiling shooter, Jenna saw a bullet slice through Cal's shirtsleeve. Bits of fabric fluttered through the air.

"Get down," she yelled, knowing it was too late and that he wouldn't listen.

Cal leaned out even farther past the cover of the doorway and sent a barrage of gunfire at the shooter in the hall. If Cal was hurt, he showed no signs of it, and there wasn't any blood on his shirt. He was in control and doing what was necessary.

Jenna knew she had to do the same.

She took a deep breath, aimed her gun at the ceiling and fired. She kept firing until the magazine was empty, and then she reloaded.

There was no sign of life. No sounds coming from above. She kept her gun ready, snatched the phone from the end table and pressed the intercom function.

"They might come through the attic," she shouted into the phone. She hoped the warning wouldn't give away Sophie's location.

Jenna tossed the phone aside and aimed two more shots into the ceiling. On the other side of the room, Cal continued to return fire.

The gunman continued to shoot at him.

Bullets were literally flying everywhere, eating their way through the walls and furniture. The glass-top coffee table shattered, sending the shards spewing through the room.

Cal cursed. And for one horrifying moment, Jenna thought he might have been hit.

Then the bullets stopped.

Jenna peered over at Cal—he wasn't hurt, thank God—and he motioned for her to get up. Since he no longer had his attention fastened to the corridor, that meant another gunman must be dead.

But there was still at least one in the attic.

Except with the silenced guns, she no longer heard any movement there. Had the person backtracked?

Or worse—had he managed to get into the gun room?

"Meggie, are you okay?" Cal shouted in the direction of the phone. He was trying to use the intercom to communicate.

While Cal kept watch of their surroundings, Jenna scurried closer to the phone that she'd tossed aside on the floor. She, too, kept her gun ready, but she put her ear closer to the receiver.

And she held her breath, waiting. Praying. Her daughter had to be all right.

"I hear something," Meggie said. "Someone's moving in the attic above us."

Oh, God. Even if that ceiling was bulletproof, it didn't mean a person couldn't figure out a way to get through it. If that happened, Meggie and Sophie would be trapped.

Jenna put her hand over the phone receiver so that her voice wouldn't carry throughout the house. "Someone's trying to get into the gun room through the attic," she relayed to Cal.

He cursed again and reloaded. The empty

magazine clattered onto the hardwood floor amid the glass, drywall and splinters. He motioned for her to get up, and Jenna knew where they were going.

To the gun room.

It was a risk. They could be leading the other shooter directly to Sophie, but judging from Meggie's comments, he was already there.

"Take the phone off intercom," Cal mouthed. "Tell Meggie we're coming, but I don't want her to unlock the door until we get there."

That meant for those seconds, she and Cal would be out in the open hall. In the line of fire. But that was better than the alternative of putting her daughter at further risk.

Still keeping low, Jenna hurried back to the phone cradle and pushed the button to disconnect the intercom. She dialed in the number that would reach the line in the gun room. Thankfully, Meggie picked up on the first ring.

"Cal and I are on the way," she relayed. "Don't unlock the door until you're sure it's us."

"What's going on, Jenna?" Meggie demanded. "Where are Cal and Jordan?"

Jenna feared the worst about Jordan. They hadn't heard a peep from the man since the gun battle. Jordan must be hurt or worse.

Jenna heard a slight click on the line, and knew what it meant. Someone had picked up another extension and was listening in.

"I can't talk now," Jenna said to Meggie, hoping the woman wasn't as close to panic as she sounded. "Just stay put…in the pantry. We'll be there soon."

She hung up and snared Cal's gaze. "Someone picked up one of the other phones."

Cal nodded.

Jenna hoped the lie would buy them some time so they could get inside the gun room. She got up so she could join Cal at the doorway.

"We do this back to back again. And hurry," he whispered. "It won't take the gunman long to figure out that they're not in the pantry."

Jenna raced toward him and got into position. She would cover the left end of the corridor. He'd cover the right just in case the gunman was still in place. They had at least thirty feet of open space between them and the gun room.

However, before either of them could move, something crashed behind them. They turned, but somehow got in each other's way.

And that mistake was a costly one.

Because the ski-mask-wearing man who broke through the doors on the other side of the family room started shooting at them.

Chapter Sixteen

Cal shoved Jenna out of the doorway and into the corridor. She'd have bruises from the fall, maybe even a broken bone, but her injuries would be far worse if he didn't get her out of there.

He dove out as well, somehow dodging the spray of bullets that the gunman was sending right at them. He barely managed to hang on to his guns.

This wasn't good. Either the guy in the attic had gotten to them ridiculously quickly, or there were more men in the house than they knew.

Cal didn't dwell on that, though. With his gun ready in his right hand, he caught Jenna with his left and dragged her to her feet. He got them moving, not a second too soon. Another round of shots fired, all aimed at them. Because he had no choice, Cal pushed Jenna into the first room they reached.

It was a guest room. Empty, he determined from his cursory glance of the darkened area. Thankfully, there was a heavy armoire against the wall between the family room and this room. That meant there was a little cushion between them and the shooter.

Cal positioned Jenna behind him and got ready to fire. "Other than where we're standing, is there any another way to access this room?" he whispered.

She groaned softly, and the sound had a raw and ragged edge to it. "Yes."

Hell. He was afraid she would say that. "Where?"

"There's a small corridor off the family room," she explained, also in a whisper. "It leads to that door over there."

Cal risked glancing across the room. He figured it was too much to hope that it would be locked or, better yet, blocked in some way. But maybe that didn't matter—this gunman had a penchant for knocking down doors.

He peered around the door edge, saw the shooter and pulled back just as another shot went flying past him.

Well, at least they knew the shooter's

location: inside the family room. "Make sure
that door over there is locked," he instructed.
"And drag something in front of it."

He'd keep the shooter occupied so that he
didn't backtrack and go after them. Of
course, that wouldn't do much to neutralize
the one in the attic.

"Jenna?" someone called out.

It was Meggie. It took Cal a moment to
realize her voice had come over the central
intercom. Anyone in the house could hear
her. Hopefully, they hadn't already pinpointed her location.

Cal glanced at Jenna, to warn her not to
answer.

"Someone's trying to get in here,"
Meggie said.

Sophie was crying. She sounded scared.
She probably was. It broke Cal's heart to
know he couldn't get to her and soothe her.

God knew what this was doing to Jenna.
The sound of her baby's tears had to be
agony. This was a nightmare that would
stay with her.

Cal wanted to check on her, but he needed
to see if anyone was in front of that gun room
door. It was a risk. But it was one he had to take.

He took a deep breath and tried to keep his

wrist loose so he could shift his gun in either direction. He leaned out slightly, angling his eyes in the direction of the gun room. No one was there, which probably meant someone was still trying to get through the attic. He didn't have time to dwell on that, though.

A bullet sliced across Cal's forearm. His shooting arm. Fire and pain spiked through him, but he choked it back and took cover.

But for only a split second.

With the sound of Sophie's cries echoing in the corridor and his head, Cal came right back out with both guns ready, and started shooting. He didn't stop until he heard the sound he'd been listening for.

The sound of someone dying.

Still, he didn't take any chances. While keeping watch all around them, he eased out of the room and walked closer until he could see the fallen gunman on the floor. His aim had hit its mark.

The guy was dead all right. The bullet in his head had seen to that. His eyes were fixed in a lifeless, blank stare at the ceiling.

Cal glanced up and listened, wanting to hear the position of the fifth and hopefully final gunman. He heard something. But the sound hadn't come from the attic. It'd come from the guest room where he'd left Jenna to block the door.

Hell.

He sprinted toward her, aimed his gun and prayed that the only thing he'd see was her trying to block that other door leading from the family room.

But that door was wide open.

Jenna was there, amid the shadows. Her face said it all. Something horrible had happened.

It took Cal a moment to pick through the shadows. Someone was standing behind Jenna.

And whoever it was had a gun pointed at her head.

JENNA REFUSED TO PANIC.

Her precious baby was crying for her. And Jenna wanted nothing more than to make sure that Sophie was okay. But she couldn't move, thanks to the ski-mask-wearing monster who'd come through the door off the family room.

It'd only taken the split-second distraction of Sophie's crying and the shots Cal had fired. Jenna had been listening to make sure he was okay. And because of that, she hadn't been watching the door. The gunman had literally walked through it and grabbed her. The gun had been put to her head before she'd even had time to react.

Now that mistake might get them both killed.

Cal stopped in the doorway, and Jenna watched him assess the situation. Either this person was going to kill them both, or he'd try to force them to give him access to the gun room.

That wasn't going to happen. Which meant they might die right here, right now.

"I'm sorry," Jenna said to Cal.

He didn't answer. He kept volleying his attention between her and the corridor, looking for the guy who'd been in the attic. Of course, that gunman could be the very person who now had a semiautomatic jammed to her head.

"I'm in here!" the guy behind Jenna suddenly yelled out. He ripped off his ski mask and shoved it into his jacket pocket. "Get down here now!"

Except it wasn't a man.

It was Helena Carr.

Jenna hadn't known whom to expect on the other end of that gun. Holden, Hollywood, Gwen and Helena had all been possibilities. All had motives, though they hadn't seemed clear. But obviously Helena's motive was powerful enough to make her want to kill.

"I'm stating the obvious here," she said, "but if either of you makes any sudden moves, I'll kill you where you stand."

"You're planning to do that anyway," Cal tossed back at her.

"Not yet. You're going to give me that screaming baby, and then you'll die very quick, painless deaths."

Oh, God. It was true. She wanted Sophie. Thankfully, her little girl's sobs were getting softer. Jenna could hear Meggie trying to soothe her, and it appeared to be working.

"Why are you doing this?" Jenna demanded.

"Lots of reasons." That was the only answer Helena gave before she started maneuvering Jenna toward the door where Cal was standing.

"Put down your guns," Helena ordered. "All of them."

Cal dropped the one from his right hand. He studied Helena's expression as she came closer. He must have seen something he didn't like because he dropped the other one, too.

Jenna's heart dropped to the floor with those weapons.

Cal wouldn't have any trouble defeating Helena if it came down to hand-to-hand combat, but Helena wasn't going to let it get to that point. She would use Jenna as a human shield to get into that gun room. Worse, she had a henchman nearby. After all, Helena had called out to someone.

With Jenna at gunpoint and Cal unarmed, this could turn ugly fast. It was a long shot, but she had to try to reason with Helena.

"Why do you want my baby?" Jenna asked. She hated the tremble in her voice. Hated that she didn't feel as in charge and powerful as Helena. She desperately wanted the power to save Sophie.

"I don't *want* your baby." Helena shoved her even closer to Cal. "But I need to tie up some loose ends."

So this was about Paul's estate. He'd left Helena some diabolical instructions as to what to do to her in the event of his death.

"I didn't do anything to hurt Paul," Jenna pleaded. "There's no reason for you to seek revenge for him."

"I'm not doing this for Paul."

Jenna heard footsteps behind her.

Helena's associate pulled off his ski mask and crammed it into his pocket. He was a bulky-shouldered man with edgy eyes. A hired gun, waiting to do whatever Helena told him to do.

"What?" Cal questioned Helena. "You don't have the stomach to kill us yourself?"

Jenna couldn't see the woman's expression, but from the soft sound that Helena made, she probably smiled. "I've killed as many men as you have—including Paul when I learned he was sleeping with both Gwen Mitchell and Jenna. The man had the morals of an alley cat."

"He slept with me to get his hands on my business," Jenna pointed out. "And Gwen slept with him to get a story. There was no affection on his part."

"That doesn't excuse it. I'm the one who set up your meeting with Paul. I'm the one who suggested he marry you so he could inherit your estate. Sleeping with you and getting you pregnant was never part of the bargain. He was supposed to marry you, drug you and then lock you away until the time was right to eliminate you completely."

"So why kill us? Why take Sophie?" Cal demanded.

Jenna could have sworn the woman's smile widened. "Oh, I don't want to take her. With my brother out of the way, I can inherit Paul's entire estate. Once any other heirs have been eliminated."

Helena's threat pounded in Jenna's head.

She wasn't going to kidnap Sophie. She was going to kill her.

That wasn't going to happen. Rage roared through her. This selfish witch wasn't going to lay one hand on her child.

"Kill Agent Rico," Helena ordered the gunman.

Jenna heard herself yell. It sounded feral, and she felt more animal than human in that moment. She didn't care about the gun to her head. She didn't care about anything other than protecting Sophie and Cal.

She rammed her elbow into Helena's stomach and turned so she could grab the woman's wrist. Jenna dug her fingernails into Helena's flesh and held on.

A bullet tore past her.

Not aimed at her, she realized. The shot had come from the gunman, and it'd been aimed at Cal.

Jenna couldn't see if Cal was all right. Helena might have had a pampered upbringing, but she fought like a wildcat, clawing and scratching at Jenna. It didn't matter. Jenna didn't feel any pain. She only felt rage, and she used it to fuel her fight all while praying that Cal had managed to survive that shot.

The gunman re-aimed.

"It's me," someone shouted. Jordan. He was alive.

That only gave Jenna more strength. She latched on to Helena with both hands and shoved the woman right at her accomplice. But the gunman got off another shot.

It seemed as if everything froze.

The bullet echoed. It was so loud that it stabbed through her head and blurred her vision. But Jenna didn't need clear vision to see the startled look on Helena's face.

The woman dropped her gun and pressed her hand to her chest. When she drew it back, her palm was soaked with her own blood. Her hired gun had accidentally shot her.

Helena smiled again as if amused at the irony. But the smile quickly faded, and she sank in a limp heap next to her gun.

Jenna forced her attention away from the woman. But she didn't have time to stop the gunman from taking aim at Cal again.

Another shot slammed past her, so close that she could have sworn she felt the heat from the bullet. A second later, she heard the deadly thud of someone falling to the floor.

The echo in her head was already unbearable and this blast only added to it. That, and the realization that Cal could be hurt.

Or dead.

She felt tears burn her eyes and was afraid to look, terrified of what she might see.

But Cal was there, his expression mirroring hers.

"I'm alive," Jenna assured him.

So was he.

He raced to her and pulled her into his arms.

Chapter Seventeen

Cal tried not to wince as the medic put in the first stitch on his right arm.

He'd refused a painkiller. Not because he was alpha or enjoyed the stinging pain. He just wanted to speed up the process. It seemed to be taking forever. He had other things to do that didn't involve stitching a minor gunshot wound.

"Hurry," he told the bald-headed medic again.

The medic snorted and mumbled something that Cal didn't care to make out. Instead, he listened for the sound of Jenna's voice. The last he saw of her, Kowalski was leading her out of the family room so he could question her.

Cal wasn't sure Jenna was ready for that. He certainly wasn't. Cal needed to see her, to make sure she wasn't on the verge of a meltdown. But Kowalski had ordered him to get stitches first. Cal had figured that would take five minutes, tops, but it'd taken longer than that just for the medic to get set up.

He heard footsteps and spotted Jordan in the doorway. The man looked like hell. There was a cut on his jaw that would need stitches, another on his head and he probably had a concussion.

Still, Jordan was alive, and an hour ago, Cal hadn't thought that was possible.

A fall had literally saved him. Jordan had explained that he'd climbed onto the gatehouse roof to stop the attack, but one of the gunmen had shot him. A minor scrape, like Cal's. But the impact of the shot had caused Jordan to fall off the roof, and he'd lain on the ground unconscious through most of the attack.

It was a different story for Jordan's assistant. Cody had been shot in the chest and was on his way in an ambulance to the hospital.

Of course, Cody was lucky just to be alive. Their attackers had obviously thought they'd killed him or else they would have put another bullet in him.

"All the gunmen are dead and accounted for," Jordan relayed.

"What about Jenna?" Cal wanted to know.

"Still talking to Kowalski in the kitchen." Jordan looked down the hall. "But you're about to get a visitor."

Cal winced. He was going crazy here. But he changed his mind when Jordan stepped aside so that Meggie could enter. She had Sophie in her arms.

"Hurry," Cal repeated to the medic.

"I'm done," the guy snapped. He motioned for Jordan to have a seat.

Cal gladly gave up his place so he could go to Sophie. The little girl automatically reached for him, and even though he had blood splattered on his shirt, he took her and pulled her close to him. Like always, Sophie had a magical effect on him. He didn't relax exactly, but he felt some of the stress melt away.

"You've seen Jenna?" he asked Meggie.

The woman shook her head. "She's still with your boss."

Enough of that. She shouldn't have to go through an interrogation alone. Cal shifted Sophie in his arms and started for the kitchen.

"Your boss has been getting all kinds of phone calls," Meggie said, trailing along behind him. "I heard him say that the guy who works for Jordan is going to be all right."

Good. That was a start. But God knows what Jenna was going through.

Cal got to the kitchen and saw Jenna seated at the table. Kowalski was across from her, talking on the phone. Jenna had her face buried in her hands.

"Jenna?" Cal called out.

Her head snapped up, and he saw her face. No tears. Just a lot of weariness.

"You're okay," Jenna said, hurrying to him.

She gathered both Sophie and him into her arms. Her breath broke, and tears came then. Cal just held on and tried to comfort her. However, the hug was cut short—Kowalski ended his call and stared at them. God knows what the man was thinking about this intimate family embrace.

And Cal didn't care.

"Holden Carr is dead," Kowalski announced.

Cal didn't let Jenna out of his arms, but he did turn slightly so he could face the director.

"Helena murdered him before she came here with her hired guns," Kowalski continued. "It appears from some notes we found in the Hummer that she eliminated her brother so he wouldn't be competition for Paul's estate."

"That's why she wanted Sophie out of

the way," Cal mumbled, though he hated to even say it aloud. He had seen the terror in Jenna's eyes when she realized what Helena wanted to do. Cal had felt the same terror in his heart.

The director nodded. "Helena was going to set up Hollywood to take the blame."

"And what about Gwen Mitchell?" Jenna asked. "Did she have anything to do with this?"

"Doesn't look that way. She just wanted a story. Helena did everything else. She planted the tracking devices on your cars. Tried to run you off the road. Faked e-mails from Paul and sent Salazar after you. Helena wanted to get you and your daughter out of the way."

So it'd all been for money. No hand from the grave. No rogue agent. Just a woman who wanted to inherit two estates and not have to share it with anyone.

"With Helena dead, the threat to Sophie is over?" Jenna asked. Cal reached over and wiped a tear from her cheek.

"It's over. You and your daughter are safe." Kowalski tipped his head toward Cal's stitches. "How about you? Are you okay?"

"Yeah." Cal had already decided what to say, and he didn't even hesitate. "But I'm not going to stay away from Jenna and Sophie."

Kowalski made a noncommittal sound and reached into his jacket pocket. "That's the letter from the promotion committee. Read it and get back to me with your decision."

"I don't have to read it. I'm not going to stay away from them."

"Suit yourself." Kowalski strolled closer. "There's no reason for me to continue with that order. Ms. Laniere is no longer in your protective custody. What you two do now is none of my business."

It took Cal a moment to realize the director was backing down. There was no reason Cal couldn't see Jenna. Well, no legal reason, anyway. It was entirely possible that Jenna would want him gone just so she could have a normal life.

Cal couldn't give her normal.

But maybe he could give her something else.

Kowalski walked out, and Cal realized that Jenna, Sophie and he were alone. Meggie had left, too. Good. Cal had some things to say, and he needed a little privacy.

He was prepared to beg.

Cal looked at Sophie first. "I want to be your dad. What do you say to that?"

Sophie just grinned, cooed and batted at his face.

He nodded. "I'll take that as a yes." He kissed the little girl's cheek and turned to Jenna.

"Yes," she said before he could open his mouth.

"Yes?" he questioned.

"Yes, to whatever you're asking." But then her eyes widened. "Unless you're asking if you can leave. Then the answer to that is no."

This had potential.

"Wait," Jenna interrupted before he could get out what he wanted to say. "I've just put you in an awkward position, haven't I?" She glanced at the letter. "You'll want to leave if you didn't get the promotion."

"Will I?"

She nodded. "Because it'll be my fault that you lost it. You resent me. Maybe not now. But later. And when you look at me, you'll think of what I cost you."

Cal frowned. "In less than a minute, you've covered a couple months, maybe even years, of our future. But for now, I'd like to go back to that yes."

"What about the letter?" she insisted. "Don't you want to know if you got the promotion?"

"Not especially."

But Jenna did. She snatched the letter from

the table, opened it and unfolded it so that it was in his face. Cal scanned through it.

"I got the promotion," he let her know. Then he wadded up the letter and tossed it.

Jenna's mouth opened, and she looked at him as if he'd lost his mind. "Don't you want the promotion?"

"Sure. But it's on the back burner right now. I'm going to ask you something, and I want you to say yes again."

She glanced at the letter, at Sophie and then him. "All right," Jenna said hesitantly.

"Will you make love with me?"

Jenna blinked. "Now?"

Cal smiled, leaned down and kissed her gaping mouth. "Later. I'm just making sure the path is clear."

"Yes." Jenna sealed that deal with a kiss of her own.

"Will you move to San Antonio with me so I can take this promotion?"

"Yes." There was no hesitation. He got another kiss. A long, hot one.

Hmmm. Maybe he could talk Meggie into watching Sophie while they sneaked off to the bedroom. But Cal rethought that. He intended to make love to Jenna all right, but he wasn't looking for a quickie. He wanted to take the time to do it right. To savor her. To let her know just how important she was to him.

And that led him to his next question. "Will you marry me?"

Tears watered her eyes. "Yes."

Cal knew this was exactly what he wanted. Sophie and Jenna. A ready-made family that was his.

"Now it's your turn to answer some questions," Jenna said. "Are you sure about this?"

"Yes." He didn't even have to think about it. "Why?"

Cal blinked. "Why?" he questioned.

"Yes. Why are you sure? Because I know why I am. I'm in love with you."

Oh. He got it now. Jenna wanted to hear the words, and Cal wasn't surprised at all that he very much wanted to say them.

He eased Jenna's hand away and kissed her. "I'm sure I love you both," Cal told them. "And I'm sure I want to be with you both forever."

Jenna smiled, nodded. "Good. Because I want forever with you, too."

It was perfect. All the yeses. The moment. The love that filled his heart. The looks on Jenna's and Sophie's faces. It wasn't exactly quiet and intimate with Sophie there, batting at them and cooing, but that only made it more memorable.

Because for the first time in his life, Cal had everything he wanted, right there in his arms.

* * * * *

TEXAS PATERNITY:
BOOTS AND BOOTIES
continues next month with
SECRET DELIVERY,
only from Delores Fossen and
Harlequin Intrigue!

Harlequin is 60 years old,
and Harlequin Blaze is celebrating!
After all, a lot can happen in 60 years,
or 60 minutes…or 60 seconds!
Find out what's going down in Blaze's
heart-stopping new miniseries,
FROM 0 TO 60!
Getting from "Hello" to "How was it?"
can happen fast….

Here's a sneak peek at the first book,
A LONG, HARD RIDE
by Alison Kent
Available March 2009

"IS THAT FOR ME?" Trey asked.

Cardin Worth cocked her head to the side and considered how much better the day already seemed. "Good morning to you, too."

When she didn't hold out the second cup of coffee for him to take, he came closer. She sipped from her heavy white mug, hiding her grin and her giddy rush of nerves behind it.

But when he stopped in front of her, she made the mistake of lowering her gaze from his face to the exposed strip of his chest. It was either give him his cup of coffee or bury her nose against him and breathe in. She remembered so clearly how he smelled. How he tasted.

She gave him his coffee.

After taking a quick gulp, he smiled and said, "Good morning, Cardin. I hope the floor wasn't too hard for you."

The hardness of the floor hadn't been the

problem. She shook her head. "Are you kidding? I slept like a baby, swaddled in my sleeping bag."

"In my sleeping bag, you mean."

If he wanted to get technical, yeah. "Thanks for the loaner. It made sleeping on the floor almost bearable." As had the warmth of his spooned body, she thought, then quickly changed the subject. "I saw you have a loaf of bread and some eggs. Would you like me to cook breakfast?"

He lowered his coffee mug slowly, his gaze as warm as the sun on her shoulders, as the ceramic heating her hands. "I didn't bring you out here to wait on me."

"You didn't bring me out here at all. I volunteered to come."

"To help me get ready for the race. Not to serve me."

"It's just breakfast, Trey. And coffee." Even if last night it had been more. Even if the way he was looking at her made her want to climb back into that sleeping bag. "I work much better when my stomach's not growling. I thought it might be the same for you."

"It is, but I'll cook. You made the coffee."

"That's because I can't work at all without caffeine."

"If I'd known that, I would've put on a pot as soon I got up."

"What time *did* you get up?" Judging by the sun's position, she swore it couldn't be any later than seven now. And, yeah, they'd agreed to start working at six.

"Maybe four?" he guessed, giving her a lazy smile.

"But it was almost two…" She let the sentence dangle, finishing the thought privately. She was quite sure he knew exactly what time they'd finally fallen asleep after he'd made love to her.

The question facing her now was where did this relationship—if you could even call it *that*—go from here?

* * * * *

Cardin and Trey are about to find out that great sex is only the beginning….
Don't miss the fireworks!
Get ready for
A LONG, HARD RIDE
by Alison Kent
Available March 2009,
wherever Blaze books are sold.

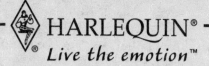

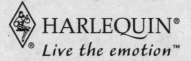

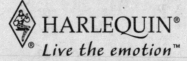

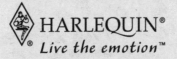

HARLEQUIN®
Presents

**The world's bestselling romance series...
The series that brings you your favorite authors,
month after month:**

Helen Bianchin...Emma Darcy
Lynne Graham...Penny Jordan
Miranda Lee...Sandra Marton
Anne Mather...Carole Mortimer
Melanie Milburne...Michelle Reid

and many more talented authors!

Wealthy, powerful, gorgeous men...
Women who have feelings just like your own...
The stories you love, set in exotic, glamorous locations...

HARLEQUIN®
Presents

Seduction and Passion Guaranteed!

HPDIR08

Harlequin® Historical
Historical Romantic Adventure!

*Imagine a time of chivalrous
knights and unconventional ladies,
roguish rakes and impetuous
heiresses, rugged cowboys
and spirited frontierswomen——
these rich and vivid tales will
capture your imagination!*

*Harlequin Historical...
they're too good to miss!*